FRIENDS IN THE WORLD

Books by Aram Saroyan

POETRY

Aram Saroyan, 1968
Pages, 1969
Words & Photographs, 1970
Cloth: An Electric Novel, 1971
The Rest, 1971
Poems, 1972
O My Generation and Other Poems, 1976

PROSE

The Street: An Autobiographical Novel, 1974
Genesis Angels: The Saga of Lew Welch & the Beat Generation, 1979
Last Rites: The Death of William Saroyan, 1982
William Saroyan, 1982
Trio: Portrait of an Intimate Friendship, 1985
The Romantic, 1988
Friends in the World: The Education of a Writer, 1992

A MEMOIR BY ARAM SAROYAN

Friends in the World

THE EDUCATION OF A WRITER

COFFEE HOUSE PRESS :: MINNEAPOLIS :: 1992

Parts of this book first appeared, often in different form, in the
following publications, to whose editors and publishers grateful
acknowledgement is made: *The American Poetry Review, Ararat,
Mother Jones, The New York Times, Nice to See You: Homage to Ted
Berrigan* (Coffee House Press, 1991), *Oculist Witnesses, The Pacific
Sun,* and *The Threepenny Review.*

Thanks go to the following foundations and corporations for
support of this project: The Bush Foundation, Minnesota State
Arts Board, Northwest Area Foundation, and Star Tri-
bune/Cowles Media Company. The publisher acknowledges the
Mary McCarthy Literary Trust for use of a brief quote in the
foreword.

Coffee House Press books are available to bookstores through
our primary distributor, Consortium Book Sales & Distribution,
287 East Sixth Street, Suite 365, Saint Paul, Minnesota 55101. Our
books are also available through all major library distributors and
jobbers, and through most small press distributors, including
Bookpeople, Bookslinger, Inland, and Small Press Distribution.
For personal orders, catalogs, or other information, write to:
COFFEE HOUSE PRESS
27 North Fourth Street, Suite 400, Minneapolis MN 55401

Library of Congress Cataloging-in-Publication Data
Saroyan, Aram.
    Friends in the World : the education of a writer : a memoir / by
    Aram Saroyan.
        p. cm.
    ISBN 0-918273-97-8 (paper) : $11.95
    1. Saroyan, Aram — Biography. 2. Authors, American — 20th century-
Biography. I. Title.
PS3569.A72Z464 1992
818'.5409 — dc20
                                                                92-3598
9 8 7 6 5 4 3 2 1   CIP

CONTENTS

To Strawberry, Cream, and Armenak
with love

FOREWORD

"For me," wrote Mary McCarthy, "the mark of the historic is the nonchalance with which it picks up an individual and deposits him in a trend, like a house playfully moved by a tornado." She is speaking of her generation's experience with communism, but her words seem to me an accurate reflection, too, of my own generation's experience during the sixties. There was a moment during that epoch when one seemed to catch the roar of history, like the sea's roar discerned in a seashell, in the random particulars of the passing scene. There is an exhilaration implicit in such a moment—to be turning, as it were, with the tide—and the years since the sixties have made it clear how rare such a moment is. If it happens in one's lifetime, it marks one, for better or worse, with the memory of a special passage in which the private and public spheres seem to merge. Indeed, what one remembers best of the period was the sense of community, of common ground, that could be spoken between strangers with a glance.

Coming of age during the sixties gave to this writer a heightened sense of being a witness. At the same time, as the distinction between the private and public spheres blurred to the edge of dissolution, it seemed possible to read broader history in the lines of one's own individual odyssey. For a writer, this notion has obvious dangers, of course, and one may argue with it even as one acts on it. "Our doubt *is* our passion," wrote Henry James. Someone else said, "It comes with the territory."

I grew up in the last generation for whom writers and poets were the genuine culture heroes. The corner paperback rack in a New York City drugstore was likely to contain serious literature in those days before the takeover of the mega-book. Then, in high school, the phenomenon of the Beat Generation occurred — echoed in England by the novelists and playwrights known as the Angry Young Men. There wasn't a serious contemporary I knew who wasn't engaged by all this.

The idea of being a writer in the late fifties or early sixties was as engaging a possibility — if, in the end, a less likely one — as being a rock musician is today. And we looked to our poets and novelists much as kids today look to their rock stars — for the truth about life.

As the child of a broken marriage, troubled by having a famous father with a public image that seemed the opposite of his private reality, I was in search of some kind of fundamental understanding upon which to base my own development. I had an uneasy sense of being estranged not only from the reality around me but from my own deeper reality as well. The situation now seems to me to have had much to do with my being the child of a public figure and wanting to be in consensus with the public's view of my father. It was a classic doublebind. If I accepted the reality of my father as I knew him, I had to do battle with the whole public perception of who he was. If, on the other hand, I tried to agree with the public perception of my parent, I would have to close off my own actual knowledge of who he was, and, by extension, who I myself was.

I turned to writing, then, as a possible means of coming to grips with the emotional confusion of my situation. I wanted to sort things out. This would be a slow process, in the end, and it would be actively complicated by the myth of a literary life.

This book traces the journey and remembers some of the people who made it come to life, taking on — with the surge of the sixties — unexpected meaning and motion of its own.

The Light in
New York

New York City, 1958. Photo by Aram Saroyan.

I read *Crime and Punishment*, for a summer assignment from Trinity School, the summer I was sixteen. I assume it was an assignment—I can't imagine I would have read it by choice because I liked much shorter books. I had a Bantam Classic paperback edition of the book, one with very thin, translucent pages, and as I read I would often notice the ratio between the number of pages read and those still to come: the thickness of the left side as compared with the thickness of the right.

That summer I worked as an office boy for Arnold Krakower, a lawyer and a family friend. He had an office on East 53rd Street between Fifth and Madison. It was air-conditioned, but I frequently went outside into the heat to deliver messages or make pickups.

Raskolnikov and I did share something, now that I think about it: the awful privacy of our outlook. I felt, essentially, ethereal, not quite all there. And yet I supposed I looked normal enough on first glance not to be called out and taken to task for my lack of full-scale reality. This was my secret. Raskolnikov, of course, had the secret of his terrible deed—his problem was, perhaps, an excess of self, the opposite of mine. But the attitude each of us brought to the ongoing spectacle of the streets seemed to me somehow similar. We were each strangers. We ate and breathed and slept our strangeness.

One of my jobs at Arnold's office was to clean my boss's law books, a chore that had been neglected for decades, and in the process of shaking the black soot from the tops of these heavy, leather-bound volumes, I inhaled the accumulation itself over and over again. After a few hours of this, my nostrils would be black, almost like a coal miner's, and I needed extra time to wash up in the bathroom at the office.

I usually had lunch at the Chock Full o' Nuts at the corner of Madison and 54th Street. Food, it was stated, untouched by human hands. (*The New Yorker* came out with a cartoon depicting the restaurant, and immediately below, in the basement, a bunch of chimpanzees putting together the sandwiches.) It was said, too, that Chock Full o' Nuts had unique hiring practices. All the branches I had ever gone into had black people behind the counters. But I heard that uptown, in Harlem, only white people were hired to serve the clientele. This still strikes me as business-wise bordering on demonic, but in practice it made only the slightest, mildest impression.

Eating a sandwich in Chock Full o' Nuts was about as close as you could come to eating it on the run in the street. One sat surrounded by strangers, all intent on their food and their *New York Times* or *New York Post.* The counters were arranged in rows, and the picture windows made the city outside at least as vivid a presence as any in the room, with the possible exception of the air-conditioning. The place was kept very cool. Entering through the revolving door, one knew instantly, and with genuine relief, that one had escaped the heat. And yet by the end of the brief meal, one almost looked forward to going back outside, to being enveloped by the heat again.

I've always liked the New York summer; the heat is a genuine common denominator, and the soul loosens in-side—even the silent, watchful soul of the screwed-up sixteen-year-old I was. I took comfort in the heat of the New York streets at least partly, I think, because it was something I shared unequivocally with everybody on them.

On the subway, I'd read a paragraph or two about Ras-kolnikov in the previous century in Russia. His intellect, his anger, his madness against the gigantic Russian air. The train roared through its tunnel, and I would pause after reading this minuscule bit and look up at my fellow passengers, knowing I'd taken just the slightest further step into the saga, and for the moment satisfied.

I washed up carefully again when I went home to my mother's little apartment on East 93rd Street between Madison and Park. For that summer when I read that first big book of my life, I had a girlfriend, the first of my life, too. At least I thought of her as a girlfriend. We were strangers, utter, irreducible strangers. But then, I was a stranger to myself.

It was a kind of black chaos that I knew inside. That was my real secret, the substance—something like the black soot on the book tops—of the strangeness I felt. My parents had both been orphans who married, divorced, married, and divorced again, all by the time I was eight. My father was a famous writer, but to me his sporadic visits were only a kind of random harassment. He had no idea how to be a father—for he himself hadn't had a father—and yet the most "public" fact about me was that I was his son.

It was as though I had half a mind. The other half was tied up, in a kind of clutch with itself, searching for what it would only find in an outward act of attention—a letting go. But I was contorted, and saw only a little of what was out there.

Yet, somehow, the city itself came through to me. I was a child of Manhattan, and the light on the buildings along Fifth Avenue in the late afternoon could send a pleasurable tremor through me. It's funny—I've only recognized this consciously in the last year or so, more than twenty years later. I loved Manhattan, the heartbreaking clarity of its light. I loved to walk its streets, the loveliest form of introspection I knew.

Let me quote something from *John Jay Chapman and His Letters,* a book I found recently in a secondhand shop on

Clement Street in San Francisco, and knew to buy for
having read about it in Edmund Wilson's *The Triple Think-
ers*. Chapman writes:

> New York is not a civilization; it is a railway station.
> There are epochs of revolution and convulsion — times of
> the migration or expulsion of races, when too much hap-
> pens in a moment to permit of anything being either un-
> derstood or recorded. Such times have no history. They
> are mysterious. Such an epoch has been passing over New
> York City ever since I have known it. The present in New
> York is so powerful that the past is lost. There is no past.
> Not a book-shelf, nor a cornice, nor a sign, nor a face, nor
> a type of mind endure for a generation.

That appeared in a book called *Emerson and Other Essays*
in 1898, yet it struck an immediate chord with me. This past
year I've gone back to the city on business three times, and
two things became clear on those visits. The simpler one —
though it came second — was the light. It was still there,
and I recognized now that it had been the deepest education of the place for me. Chapman is right. There is no past
in Manhattan, no enduring tradition. However, there is
Madison Avenue, Fifth Avenue, and Central Park. And
there is twilight. And noon. The city sparkles, regularly.
And this is what reached me, again and again, and imparted
delight. In other words, the city's lessons were a kind of
poetry, and dangerous in that sense, too.

The other thing I learned on my visits during this past
year, the thing that struck me first, is that the city — surprise! — is really all about money, a huge, light-splintering
financial engine, constantly revving itself. What had happened to me as an adolescent, I realized one bright morning
last fall on Madison Avenue, is that art — which, after all, is
only a single, relatively insignificant aspect of the reality of
New York, a sort of window dressing on the main action — had caught my eye, and I had mistaken its magne-
tism for a sign of its preeminence in the general scheme of

things. What I had missed, as a result, was that the building with the ground floor windows featuring an original drawing by Matisse and a pastel on canvas by Berthe Morisot was built and owned by business with no connection to the ground floor display. I missed the forest for the trees, you might say. The art dealers and gallery owners were the renters, for the most part; and the builders and owners gave them the street-level window displays as a practicality, not as a sign of any special allegiance.

But the self-involved adolescent, walking up and down the Avenue, saw only the freedom of the hand of Matisse, the bold strokes of Morisot, and missed most of the rest. I found in Manhattan a smaller — if to me more vividly compelling — world than the one that made up the rules. My mistake. I would be years learning those rules which many, raised under less special circumstances and in a less accelerated environment, have accepted as a matter of course by the time they reach their majority. From my Manhattan adolescence, I emerged not the hard-nosed, practiced customer so often identified with the city, but with the rarified credentials of an Upper East Side aesthete, credentials that would need to be drastically supplemented before they would prove negotiable in the world.

And yet, as I thought that morning last October even in the midst of the reckoning, what a luminous light the city showed me. What prodigies of intense private experience I knew in the days of my New York rounds. And what value it would all have, once I learned to make ends meet in the larger world. Having made the decision to be a writer, it took me time to discover that a private and a public self were not mutually exclusive, but as complementary as sunlight and shadow on Madison Avenue.

The Upper East Side
State of Mind

Steve Reichman, Trinity School, 1962.

I

Roy Cohn, the attorney and former aide to Senator Mc-
Carthy, gave the eulogy at Steven Reichman's funeral in
the fall of 1964 at a funeral home in midtown Manhattan.
Then, after Cohn spoke, Charles Mingus, unannounced
and unseen behind the proscenium curtain, played a slow,
mournful bass solo in honor of his young friend and fan,
who had died that summer in Tangier. He was nineteen
years old when he died, an Upper East Side boy who had
graduated from Trinity School and was attending New
York University. The juxtaposition of Roy Cohn, in
front, and Charlie Mingus, behind the curtain, still seems,
more than twenty years later, a perfect symbolic embodi-
ment of the paradox at the heart of Steve Reichman's short
life.

Two years younger than I, he had an even-featured,
gentle-humored face with close-cropped curly brownish
blond hair. We'd become friends during my last years of
high school; then, the summer before I started college at
the University of Chicago, we shared a room together a
few steps down from the sidewalk under a barbershop on
East 86th Street between Second and First Avenues. Steve
had either found the place himself or inherited it from
someone. Its chief value was that for the moment there was
no rent since we were holding the landlord in a standoff
until he made certain repairs.

The room was like a long corridor and had a concrete
floor. Two army cots ran across one wall. A window
looked out on the sidewalk on one end. At the other end,
the small kitchenette followed by the doorless bathroom
with a shower stall were problematic. One problem: when
the shower was used, water flowed into the entryway just
outside the room's front door. The other problem was that

the small refrigerator didn't close, it needed to be *tied*
shut — with a blue terrycloth belt borrowed from a bath-
robe.

It was the summer of 1962. I had just graduated from
Trinity and was working as a messenger for Academy
Typing Service on Seventh Avenue just up from Fourteenth Street. Academy was owned and run by Virginia
Admiral, the former wife of the painter Robert De Niro,
Sr., and mother of the actor Robert De Niro, who was then
an adolescent who occasionally came up to the office to see
his mother. Steve, who had a year left to go at Trinity, was
working further downtown as an office boy for Roy
Cohn, whom he spoke of — albeit with an obligatory implied apology in his tone — as a decent, caring man. I dare
say that summer we were, both of us, waiting out private
limbos.

Each evening as I entered the room after work I encountered a small watercolor Steve had done and scotch-taped
to the wall above his cot. It depicted a man's face in the sun,
that was all, but it has proven one of the most memorable
works of art in my life. The subject was a fellow student at
Trinity, someone in my own class whom I disliked. But the
painting had to do with the sun and the man in such a way
that my classmate's identity wasn't at issue at all. It was
about the warmth of the sun on the face of the man; it was
about, it seemed to me, the greatness of the gift of life, in
the same way van Gogh's paintings are about it.

2

Steve's mood that summer seemed a highly sensitized de-
pression. This was complicated, I gathered, by the fact that
he was taking tranquilizers prescribed by a psychiatrist.
We didn't talk very much, or do very much together — I
don't remember even sharing a meal. We were simply the

sharers of a room who said a few words to each other from time to time. And yet there was an unspoken current of sympathy between us. To a third person I would have spoken of him as a close friend, although I now see that neither of us just then were really capable of friendship.

One Friday I got a message at Academy Typing Service to call an old neighborhood friend from California whom I'd last seen when we were fifteen and who was in town for the weekend. I needed to construct a face to meet my old friend, who was accompanied, it turned out, by a female cousin. We ended up going to a place called The Third Side on Bleecker Street where we listened to Cecil Taylor play a relentlessly pounding, exhausting, and yet, in the end, exalted, cathartic set of jazz piano. I said goodnight to my friend and his cousin in front of their downtown hotel and went back uptown to my cot under the window.

Not long after that, Steve came back to the room one evening and told me he'd lost his virginity with one of two notorious twin sisters who lived on Park Avenue. Still a virgin, two years older and a little taller than him, I was put off by the news. I made a callous, disparaging remark about the sisters and suddenly he pushed me hard enough to make me fall on the concrete floor and scrape the side of my hip. I was more astonished—and chastened to have touched so deep a nerve in him—than angry. I got up, checking myself and deciding I didn't want to respond in kind. He apologized and I left the room and walked up 86th Street in the neon-bright evening.

3

That summer a place called the Psychiatric Treatment Center, a few blocks east and downtown from our room, began to figure in our lives. It was a high-priced live-in

psychiatric clinic with the privileges of a hotel that was a
home to people of our age and general milieu, young
Upper East Side problem cases. I remember a lovely slen-
der girl named Laura who visited our room and, as we sat
side by side on Steve's cot, put her hand on my thigh once
in passing, a moment that gave me infinite hope about my
future.

Laura's companion that day was Richard Needles, another resident of PTC, as it was known. Dick Needles was
a dark, intense sixteen-year-old with a mop of black hair
and an apocalyptic look in his eye. He was a student at
Riverdale, another prep school, and told us he'd climbed to
the roof of the school gym and threatened to jump. He also
said he was a writer and at work on several novels. Meeting
Dick was an event for me, since I knew no writers my age.
I wanted to be a writer, but my mind and guts were so
scrambled I despaired of having anything comprehensible
to say.

Steve was at first respectful, and then increasingly suspicious. The upshot of it was he thought Dick was grand-
standing his madness, using it socially, playing at being
crazy. This was the period of the Beat Generation and jazz
and the Angry Young Men in England, and rebellion in all
its forms, including outright madness (Artaud, for instance, was a Beat hero), was very much in currency. My
own relationship with Dick was one of thwarted anticipation. I was intrigued to know he was there, working on his
novels, and felt that a big breakthrough conversation was
in the offing between us. But somehow the conversation
never seemed to take place.

That summer at my job as a messenger I wore shoes that
were too tight, telling myself it was only a matter of time
before I broke them in. This never happened and I limped
around until my father came to town and bought me a new
pair for college. The last few days before I took the plane

for Chicago, Steve mysteriously disappeared. He never did return to the room and I didn't find out where he was until after I started classes.

4

I got a letter from him, a quiet, sane, caring letter, explaining he'd been very depressed and finally taken the step of committing himself to PTC. He had been reading *Rabbit, Run.* "What a refreshing awakener of the senses Updike is!" he wrote.

At Chicago I also began a correspondence with Dick Needles at the same address, and these letters were like that conversation I'd been waiting for. He wrote that he'd just finished reading Kerouac's *Big Sur,* which he loved, and at the same time the latest volume of Anthony Powell's *A Dance to the Music of Time,* which he didn't like. I wrote back in the same rushing, free-style manner.

For the Thanksgiving holidays I took a plane back to New York, for the first time frightened by the international scene: the Cuban Missile Crisis. By Christmas vacation I'd decided to leave Chicago for good. I wasn't really grown-up enough for college, while at the same time a poem I'd submitted that fall to David Ignatow at *the Nation* had been accepted for publication.

It wasn't long after I returned to New York, where I was living again with my mother and stepfather, that I ran into Steve in midtown on Park Avenue one sunny winter day under the huge glass office buildings. I was happy to see him again, and astonished at his growth: he had shot up overnight to six-foot-two or -three. I'm five-feet-ten-and-a-half and I'd been the taller one of us the preceding summer. He approached me smiling and said, "Listen, man, I've really got it. Listen to this."

"OK," I said and waited smiling in the cold sunshine, both our breaths visible in the air.

"Charlie Parker *thinks* faster," he said, looming over me urgently.

I thought that was pretty good myself. By now he'd started going to The Five Spot downtown off of Astor Place and was listening to Charlie Mingus, Thelonious Monk, and Sonny Rollins in live performance.

I visited him once or twice at PTC during this period. On one visit, with an only half-comic I-rest-my-case manner, he showed me a photograph he'd taken over the toilet bowl of a recent bowel movement of his that had taken the form of a perfect question mark. I wondered how much good the place could be doing him. It was like the college dormitory I'd known at Chicago except in each room one ran the risk of encountering outright madness. Since he'd been a resident, Steve had attempted suicide by slitting his wrists.

He told me he'd entered a contest that Norman Mailer ran via his monthly column in *Esquire*. Mailer asked his readers to submit essays on the theme of proving they weren't members of the FBI. Steve's piece began "I'm not a member of the FBI, I'm a patient at the Psychiatric Treatment Center," and he was mentioned by name in Mailer's follow-up column.

I also saw Dick Needles from time to time — outside of PTC, since it wouldn't have been possible to visit Steve and Dick together at the Center. They plainly disdained each other now. Dick and I attended a writers' forum in the Village one night at which Seymour Krim, among others, spoke. And Dick visited me one night at my mother and stepfather's apartment on West End Avenue. My mother encountered him as he came in and told me later she thought he looked like a drug addict.

After the winter break I'd enrolled as a freshman again at the Washington Square campus of NYU, and this time

ended up flunking out. At the Chock Full o' Nuts across
the street from the main building I reached for my coffee
one afternoon and noticed my hand was trembling.

5

That summer, during a single afternoon at the West End
Avenue apartment, I wrote the first real poems of my life,
and a day or so later went to visit Steve at his parents' beach
house on Long Island.

Mr. Reichman, Steve's father, had become very successful by working out one of the original games that super-
market chains used to lure customers. He was a trim man
with a wry manner. Mrs. Reichman was a big voluptuous
woman with an outgoing personality — an Oedipal night-
mare, Steve wanted it known. At dinner I had so much
trouble suppressing an impulse to laugh at one of his un-
derhanded comments that my left leg shot out under the
table and locked, rigid, in that position. I thought I'd have
to be carried from the table, but by the end of the meal the
leg-lock mercifully broke and I could get up.

I also visited the Reichmans' new Manhattan townhouse
off of Madison Avenue, one of the rewards of Mr. Reichman's financial killing. The living room had a spiral stair-
case, and the whole place had a quality I hadn't encountered before. Everything in it seemed simultaneously
brand-new and somehow pasted together, both expensive
and oddly lightweight. Steve was on balance sympathetic
toward his father, but he seemed to be in an all-out rebellion against what he took to be his mother's nouveau riche
impulses.

One night outside Stark's on Madison Avenue and 78th
Street he showed up on a new motorcycle. He offered me
a ride and I got onto the back. Going by Doubleday's on

Fifth Avenue and 57th Street we hit a tremendous bump that had us airborne. When we somehow came down again on our seats I immediately got off the bike.

6

I was living now in my first apartment, at 321 East 45th Street, and working at Bookmasters Bookstore on Broadway off of Times Square. Allen Ginsberg, whom I'd met, came into the store once or twice. I'd begun to follow the poetry scene, and one evening made a pilgrimage down to Le Metro coffeehouse near St. Mark's Place, where all the poets read their poems. Allen Ginsberg, Paul Blackburn, Diane Wakoski, and Jackson MacLow were just a few of the poets one might regularly find at adjoining tables. During this period Dick Needles left PTC and went off to Europe to continue his writing or expand his horizons, or both.

Occasionally I would run into Steve downtown. He was spending a lot of time now at The Five Spot, where he got to know Charlie Mingus. He also frequented a bar up the street where he played pool and took up with prostitutes who were regulars of the place. This was way beyond my ken. I was still working on my virginity. The last time I saw him I ran into him at a bar called The Ninth Circle in the West Village.

He told me that night that he'd fallen in love with a girl he'd met at NYU, where he was now a student. They'd arranged to rendezvous that summer in the south of France, although they would be going to Europe and traveling there separately.

It was only a week or so before he was to leave. His mood had lightened and he looked stronger and healthier than ever before. He described the relationship he and his girlfriend had as a very "hormonious" one. (It occurs to me now that his humor and style as a person had a lot in it of the David Addison character as played by Bruce Willis on "Moonlighting.") I wished him a good trip and looked forward to seeing him when he got back.

7

For several years I'd been frequenting an early crashpad on Grand Street, a place rented by, among one or two other perennials, a friend named Bob Stewart who ran the offset printing press at Academy Typing Service. Bob was a big bear of a man with a carefully trimmed beard and a soft, kindly voice, and he loved to play the cordial host to the comings and goings of his Village crowd. He was from Trenton, New Jersey, the son of a penitentiary warden, and eventually ended up doing time himself for a drug bust. Then, in the early eighties, he was killed in a car accident. He couldn't have been more solicitous of his friends, and he was surely among those who pioneered the lifestyle that caught on during the sixties.

It was at Bob's Grand Street railroad flat that I'd pick up periodic bits of information about Dick Needles in Europe. At one point I heard he was ill with hepatitis in Greece and there was speculation then about whether he was into drugs. I seem to have been too conservative in my own drug use — an occasional hit of marijuana, which the first dozen or so times didn't seem to affect me at all — to give much credence to these rumors.

Bob and his friends were relocating that summer from Grand Street to another place in the Village, and suddenly Dick had returned from Europe. I saw him again one night in the Village at a plushly appointed highrise apartment the Stewart crowd had managed to take over for the moment. I was eager to discuss writing with him, feeling I'd come along myself in the interim (my first poems and a review had been printed in *Poetry* the past spring). But Dick proved strangely evasive, fixing me with a half-smiling stare I couldn't make head or tail of. The upshot of the few words we exchanged that night in the highrise was that writing had receded for him as a priority and he'd done very little of it recently. My own self-absorption was so great I only half believed him and expected he soon would turn around and be my writing friend again, although by now I was getting to know other writers my age in New York. Dick told me one other thing that night, apropos a discussion of romantic prospects. He told me, with the implication that he no longer needed to exert himself on this score, either, that he was able . . . how shall I put it? . . . to bring himself to a climax orally.

"Really?" I said, incredulous.

He nodded with a half-smile.

8

One night in late summer I went into my old after-school haunt, Stark's, where one of my former classmates at Trinity, Jeff Harris, told me he was driving across the country to Los Angeles and asked if I'd like to come along. Harris and I weren't friends, but after a moment's hesitation I said yes. I wanted to be let off in Albuquerque to visit Robert Creeley, with whom I'd corresponded. I had a feeling I could learn from Creeley in person what continued to elude me in his letters, to wit, what a real poem was and how one was written on purpose.

Jeff was leaving at the crack of dawn the next morning and I agreed to be ready at my apartment on East 45th Street. Then I must have decided to stay up all night. By now, Bob Stewart's gang had relocated to an apartment on

Lafayette Street near Astor Place, and I ended up seeing Dick again there that night. After a while the two of us decided to walk over to his apartment a few blocks east on the Lower East Side.

Now we'll talk, I thought as we headed toward his place. About midway down a long block we entered a building. We walked the length of its first-floor corridor and went out the back door into a courtyard. It was long after midnight, but geared up for the trip across the country, my adrenalin was flowing. We crossed the courtyard — a thin moon visible in the sky — and entered the building on the other side of it. We took the stairs up two flights and entered Dick's apartment.

This was the first bona fide hippie pad I ever saw: mattress on the floor, Indian prints and deep red fabrics across the bed and on the wall. Dick lit a stick of incense and put on a Ravi Shankar record, keeping the sound low. He kept smiling at me with that vague expression, as if he were waiting for the particular page on my face to turn and reveal another sort of person than the one he read there at the moment.

I still wanted to talk about writing. I was a hardheaded young man of twenty at the beginning of an odyssey, and I wasn't very sensitive to nuances in my friends' behavior unless they impinged on me threateningly. I must have considered myself in a fairly secure position vis-à-vis Dick Needles just then, since he hadn't yet published anything and I had. I took a chair beside a small writing table against the wall. On the table — literally staring me in the face, had I been any less oblivious — was a spoon edged with a solidified black substance.

"What are you writing these days?" I asked Dick.

"Oh, man, I told you, I don't do that anymore."

He was now seated on the floor near my feet and had brought out several objects — found objects: a toy car, a nut

and bolt, a length of chain, that he'd picked up on neighborhood walks — and was moving them around on the
floor with one finger and looking up with his half-smile.
As I saw it, this was the peace-that-passeth-understanding
pose, a stance calculated to intimidate more driven types
such as me. But I wasn't buying it.

The tabla part of the Shankar record was happening now
and I picked up the spoon on the table and began drumming in time to it, which disturbed him.

"Hey, don't do that."

"*OK*," I said and stopped.

From time to time, both keyed-up and frustrated, I returned to the drumming, and each time he asked me to
stop. Some part of me must have enjoyed putting him off
his pose of complete contentment and engaging his irrita-
tion, which was at least more human. But I wasn't consciously trying to bother him; I only thought he was being
unnecessarily uptight about something not very important, having hardly noticed, as I say, his dope apparatus. He
did say he thought the neighbors would be disturbed by
my drumming. But as I sat looking from the table out the
window into the nighttime courtyard — a scene putting me
in mind of one of Creeley's poems — after a moment or
two, I would unconsciously begin drumming again.

Then he stood up, walked around, and suddenly his
hand came down on my drumming hand, hard, stopping
me and shocking me too.

"*Stop it,* will you?" he said with a frustrated plea in his
tone. "I'm sorry, man. But I told you not to do it."

As when Steve Reichman had pushed me to the floor of
our room, I went through the obligatory review of my
insides, wondering if I wasn't obliged to respond in kind.
But again I couldn't see it, and only got up and self-righ-
teously walked out of the apartment, down the stairs,

through the courtyard, down the corridor, and out the front door onto the street.

Well, I thought, that's the end of *that* friendship. Even though Dick had been apologetic, he just didn't seem to care about anything anymore.

Now I'd take the Astor Place subway home to do my packing before taking off with Jeff Harris in a couple of hours. As I reached the corner of the deserted street I heard a voice and turned around to see Dick running up the street after me.

"Hey, man," he said breathlessly when he got to the corner, "I'm really sorry. Really. OK? I'm really sorry."

"OK," I said.

"Have a good trip."

"Thanks."

"I didn't mean to hit you. OK?"

"OK," I said and smiled.

"OK," he said, smiling now too.

He turned around to go back to his apartment (I was silently hoping he'd be willing to see me through the rest of the night), and I turned to walk to the subway.

9

I went to New Mexico and saw Creeley. As I was showing him some of my recent poems, he said something about "hearing" one line with another a dozen or so lines later in the poem. That flipped a switch — I thought I finally understood what I needed to understand about making a poem.

I went on by bus from Placitas, and stopped in LA and saw my friend for the first time since the night of the Cecil Taylor set. Then I got a bus up to San Francisco and saw my father for a few days. Then I caught a Greyhound headed back to New York.

Robert Creeley in Placitas, New Mexico, 1964.

Maybe it was in Missoula, maybe it was outside Omaha, maybe it was over the rainbow, but one night in the crowded, darkened bus, wide-awake while seemingly everyone but the driver dozed in helter-skelter positions in their reclining seats, I suddenly felt, deep in that American night, really OK about everything. The world was OK, I was OK. Being on a bus in the middle of the night probably had something to do with it: a crowd going through nowhere — that's life, maybe?

When I got back to New York — fresh from Creeley's transmission of a poetic tradition — I put together plans to start my own little literary magazine with a small inheritance I'd come into during the past year.

It was one night soon after I got back—I no longer remember quite where or how—that I heard Steve Reichman had been discovered dead in his hotel room in Tangiers. And later the same night at the apartment on Lafayette Street, Bob Stewart nodded at my information about Steve, which he seemed to have already heard, and then asked if I'd heard about Dick Needles. When I said I hadn't, he told me Dick had had a relapse of hepatitis, apparently from using a dirty needle, and had died.

The news came so fast I didn't react emotionally at all. I was about to turn twenty-one; neither of them could have been more than nineteen. For several years I had moments when I thought I saw Dick or Steve on the street in Manhattan and would have to remind myself they were dead. Since I'd never known Dick's parents, there was no follow-up of any kind after I heard the news from Bob. Dick was just out of the picture, gone.

10

But with Steve it was different. The death was mysterious, but a consensus seemed to develop among his friends and family that it had been an accident, an unlucky mixing of tranquilizers and alcohol. Eventually his body was shipped home, and one evening before the funeral I talked on the phone with Mrs. Reichman. She told me that among Steve's belongings shipped back with his body was an unsent letter to me, and invited me to come over that night to see it.

When I saw her in her living room that night, Mrs. Reichman was visibly bereaved, and yet was making a determined effort at doing right by one of Steve's friends. I felt sorry for her and moved by her effort.

She brought out the letter from Steve in an envelope addressed to me in red ink, as was the letter itself. It was otherwise a quite ordinary looking letter, though, which shouldn't have been surprising, but it was—I guess I expected a letter from someone who had died to be somehow different. The letter described his meeting with his girlfriend in the south of France. They hadn't, it turned out, hit it off as expected and, disappointed, he'd gone on alone with his travels. The letter was written from his hotel room in Tangier. He'd been reading William Burroughs and Camus and "thinking about electric money," he wrote. I had no idea what electric money was and still don't, but that phrase was a final item in what still seems a vivid verbal legacy.

Mrs. Reichman wanted me to take the letter, but I declined, feeling she needed everything of her son's that had come back. I thanked her and, after stammering my condolences, was back on the autumn-clear sidewalk of Madison Avenue under the streetlights.

II

The funeral gathering included people I'd known a long time while growing up in Manhattan, but it passed in an emotionally indecipherable blur. Roy Cohn wasn't the right man to speak for Steve's passage on earth. Charles Mingus, by choice unseen, came much closer to the eloquence needed to make his death real. But still, Steve seemed to have slipped through virtually unfathomed.

As the years have gone by, I've encountered a surprising number of friends and acquaintances from the Upper East Side whose lives seem to have taken a strange turn. Someone I'd known well is, the last I heard, an ordained Zen priest living in Montana. Another, now in San Francisco, works from time to time as a gardener. Still another, a former drummer with a rock band, told me several years ago it was hard to bite the bullet because "the bullet come so fast." And still another once showed me the pages of his diary which seemed to be made up of layers upon layers of writing that had turned into an impenetrable scroll.

After a while it occurred to me that there may have been something heady and destabilizing in the very air we breathed growing up on the Upper East Side of New York, a special, rarified Upper East Side state of mind. It was said to be the top of the world, the place we came from, at least according to certain maps — and where were we supposed to travel from there?

Steve Reichman seemed to have embarked on an instinctive, but perhaps too accelerated journey down — toward more solid ground. Dick Needles, starting out perhaps on a similar passage, seemed to get twisted behind drugs. When they both died within a week of each other, I thought of the irony and outrage they would feel on encountering one another on the other side. Then I began to think they would have to know and understand and forgive each other at last. For though the sixties had only just begun to go into gear, each of them seemed to pick up the spirit of that period faster and more precipitously than anyone else I knew.

In the end it was as if the two men who divided the eulogy for Steve Reichman at his funeral embodied a fundamental division in his life, which would later come to be known as the generation gap. Roy Cohn spoke of and for the milieu he had inherited from his family; while Charles Mingus, choosing not to speak or be visible at the funeral's gathering of family and friends, let us hear from behind the proscenium curtain the music Steve, just in advance of the coming wave of his generation, found and took to heart on his own.

My Sixties

I

As I write, it is twenty years since the heyday of the sixties and, in a political and economic climate that is in extreme contrast to that earlier epoch, there seems to be a gathering nostalgia. The *New York Times Book Review* prints on its front page reviews of exhaustive summaries of the decade, often written by former members of the New Left who are now college professors. Television shows like "Family Ties" and "thirtysomething" have a steady undercurrent of rueful wonder at the passing of a time that seemed, for a moment, to hold the promise of the future.

I should say right away that I'm not undertaking here another summary of the period. Let me confess that I've been unable to read the recent books about the sixties or even to muster a glancing interest in most of them. I know that they are most likely about *somebody's* sixties, but I know viscerally that a four- or five-hundred-page book of small type with a forty-page section of notes and footnotes at the end isn't my sixties.

Let me put it another way. To me, "the sixties" means my youth, and the youth of the friends with whom I shared it. Here, then, in lieu of a more sweeping overview, are some notes on that time.

In the fall of 1964 I was a twenty-one-year-old college dropout who, with the help of a modest inheritance, had started a literary magazine in New York City. I lived in a ground-floor studio apartment in a highrise on East 45th Street near the United Nations building. Being a poet who had just begun to publish, I was eager to make contact with my literary contemporaries, and the little magazine was a nice entree into the milieu. Young poets need a place to publish, and the magazine gave me an excuse to make contact with anyone whose work I liked.

When the first issue of my magazine, *Lines,* came out that fall, I received a typed, single-spaced two-page letter from Ron Padgett, a young poet whose work I admired who lived on West 88th Street. The letter was long and leisurely and moderately personal; Padgett noted, for instance, that he was typing it late at night with his wife asleep in the next room. He told me he enjoyed the magazine and more or less welcomed me to the New York poetry scene.

Not long afterwards, probably at the regular Wednesday night open poetry readings at the Le Metro coffee house on the Lower East Side, I met Padgett in person. Tall and thin, twenty-two years old, with an attractive, easygoing manner, he had graduated from Columbia University where he had taken Kenneth Koch's poetry class. A native of Tulsa, Oklahoma, he had recently gotten married to a pretty, dark-haired young woman named Patty Mitchell, also from Tulsa. Beyond these biographical details, he was the boldest poet of my age around. For instance, just before I received the letter from him, I had come across a poem of his in the Tulsa-New York School house-organ of the moment, *C* magazine, edited by Ted Berrigan, a long poem entitled "A Game of Chess" that I couldn't make head or tail of and hence was obliged to take very seriously indeed.

He was, it turned out, a devotee of Marcel Duchamp and the French Surrealists and carried himself with the slightly scholarly aplomb of an old-fashioned European master of mischief: a quiet-spoken, modest man-of-letters who was going to routinely explode a lot of old hat preconceptions about what poetry was.

I remember two things he said to me during this period that may give a sense of his style. He told me one night in a gentle tone that it was one of his ambitions to publish a beautiful, expensive edition of *A Midsummer Night's Dream*

Reading at Wagner College, 1964. Left to right, Peter Orlovsky,
Joe Brainard, Gerard Malanga, Ted Berrigan, Ron Padgett.

with T. S. Eliot's name on it as the author of the play. I took
this in smiling, a little baffled, but overall intrigued by the
idea of playing such quiet, low-key havoc with the world
of letters.

About a year later, shortly after his return from a year in
Paris on a Fulbright, he told me something more personal,
indicating beforehand a friend's confidence. This would
be, now, the early summer of 1966, shortly after the release
of The Beatles' album *Revolver.*

"I would never admit this," he said one afternoon in my
apartment on West 85th Street, where I had moved in the
fall of 1965, "but between The Beatles and The Rolling
Stones, I would choose The Beatles."

This is the sort of remark I imagine is virtually a character signature for anyone who knew the sixties that we

knew, and a virtual conundrum for anyone who didn't. The Beatles, that is, were at this stage still like the rock and roll equivalent of a delicious cold glass of chocolate milk, while The Rolling Stones were more like whiskey, straight up. The Beatles were cherubs, The Stones were punks. The Beatles were husband material, The Stones were backdoor men. A little later, when the Beatles were following the Maharishi and released *The White Album,* The Stones were getting into trouble — Brian Jones would soon die of a drug overdose — and, virtually simultaneously with the release of that pristine, joyous Beatles album, they released one called *Beggar's Banquet,* beginning with the classic "Sympathy for the Devil." Later still The Beatles made an album called *Let It Be,* and The Stones answered it with one called *Let It Bleed.* One can push this contrast only so far, of course, as anyone who has kept current with Mick Jagger is aware. But I knew what Ron was saying just then and was glad he thought we were close enough for him to say it. I also appreciated and sympathized personally with what he said, since, as much as I loved The Stones, I had hopes myself of finding, not too far down the line in my life, a lasting relationship with a woman, marriage, and children.

2

If Ron Padgett, then, was in his personal life an exemplary figure to me, I found in his friend and mentor, Ted Berrigan, already thirty years old or thereabouts, a more unexpected, sometimes unnerving, vastly compelling *presence.* E. M. Forester remarks somewhere of a relationship that, by being strictly limited, it had achieved a sacred character. When I read this it immediately struck me as true of my relationship with Ted, whom I saw relatively rarely over the years.

I'm not sure when we first met, but the first vivid memory I have of Ted is at the party Frank O'Hara and Joe LeSueur gave in May of 1964 for the Italian poet Guiseppe Ungaretti, a magnificent white-haired old man. Frank and Joe's loft below Union Square on Broadway was teeming with New York poets that spring afternoon and evening. Along with Frank, there were James Schuyler, John Ashbery, Kenneth Koch, Allen Ginsberg, and LeRoi Jones, all of whom read from their work toward the end of the party. And they were followed by Ungaretti himself, who read with such thunderous passion I found myself moved despite the fact that I knew no Italian. Younger poets, though none read, were also out in force: Ed Sanders, Ron Padgett, Dick Gallup, Tony Towle, David Shapiro, Kathleen Fraser, Jack Marshall, and Jim Brodey I remember, and I'm sure there were others. At one point, Ed Sanders circulated a request for a single pubic hair from each poet in attendance. I wasn't certain how to comply, exactly, but Allen Ginsberg standing nearby quietly reached into his pants and extracted the item, enlightening me. The collection — carefully labeled in glassine envelopes — was later offered for sale to literary collectors through Sanders's Peace Eye Bookstore mail-order catalogue.

At the time, Ted Berrigan occupied a position somehow *between* the elder and the younger poets. Only shortly before the party, I had come across a copy of his legal-sized, stapled, and mimeographed magazine, *C,* at the Kornblee Gallery on the Upper East Side, and I was aware of him and his Oklahoma cohorts Ron Padgett, Dick Gallup and the painter and writer Joe Brainard, who did the *C* magazine covers, as a high-spirited band of young mavericks — though their allegiance was firmly to the New York School (O'Hara, Ashbery, Koch, etc.) — who had come to town and were in the midst of making a splash with their

talent, wit, and — not least, so far as their immediate contemporaries were concerned — effrontery. In fact, Ted was
older than the others — twenty-nine at the time, the same
age as LeRoi Jones (a year or so later Imamu Amiri Baraka),
but he was the editor of C and the group's unofficial mentor, so one tended to think of him among the younger
poets. To give a sense of a particular approach he could take
socially, I can quote a remark he made to me that afternoon.

First, though, I should say I was a native New Yorker
who, at twenty, had just made his official debut as a poet
with six poems and a review in *Poetry*. I was terribly serious
about poetry and immediately sensed that my literary
"stance," to use a word favored by the group of Black
Mountain poets I looked to (Creeley, Olson, Dorn, etc.),
wouldn't be much to Ted and his group's liking.

However, when we said hello and someone made refer-
ence to my recently published poems, Ted surprised me by
responding in a warmly positive tone. He was a bearded
bear of a man even then, but at the same time there was
something easy-natured and relaxing in his manner that
released me from the reticence I might ordinarily have felt.

"But you don't really *like* my poems, do you?" I asked.

"Oh, man," he answered in his Oklahoma accent — he
was from Providence, Rhode Island, but had gone to the
University of Tulsa on the GI Bill after Korea — "I think
they're elegant. But I wish — I wish you'd tell a few *lies* in
your poems. You know?"

I smiled at this, but I *didn't* know. And yet I liked it
somehow anyway. The Black Mountain style is a valuable,
exacting medium for a young poet, but I was apparently
ready just then to be given the keys to a more carefree
vehicle — if only for an occasional joy-ride. "My friends
and I like to tell a few jokes in our poems sometimes," Ted
added, "since we are real poets, like Frank said in his poem

Ted Berrigan at Gem Spa, St. Mark's Place & Second Avenue, New York, 1971. Photo © by Gerard Malanga.

'Why I am not a Painter.' I think you'd be good at that too." In the nicest way imaginable, Ted was telling me I might lighten up.

This was the first of many acts, tactful, sweet-natured and full of a real generosity of spirit, that I was to know him by during the next couple of years.

It was a few months later, in the fall of 1964, in the Eighth Street Bookshop, that I came across the first edition, mimeographed and staple-bound, with a photo-offset cover by Joe Brainard, of Ted's *The Sonnets,* a great sonnet series that amounts to a single song of youth and poetry and love, of New York City and friendship and amphetamine, of sweetness and clarity of heart — a classic. I bought the book and took it home, read it and loved it, and instantly wrote Ted a note.

What he had done, it seemed to me, was to combine the lyric, romantic qualities of the New York School — best exemplified by the work of his own master, Frank O'Hara — with the fine attention to sound that had up to then been the rather strict province of the Black Mountain School, my own biggest influence. Ted could go loose and still make beautiful music, and that seemed and still seems a breakthrough.

When I saw him next at Le Metro he told me my note had made his day, and our friendship began. Another dimension of his importance — I would guess for Ron, Dick Gallup and Joe Brainard as well as for me — was that here was someone almost a decade older than us who somehow or other managed to do what we wanted to do, albeit without making any noticeable money for it, but apparently none the worse for wear.

I say "apparently" because in fact the whole concept of a literary life — apart from holding a university teaching post to subsidize it — is a flagrant myth, and not necessarily a harmless one.

Yet there was Ted, right out in front of me as I began my own odyssey, and he was going about the business of being an old-fashioned man of letters. He was FACT, writ large, whatever other evidence there might be that you couldn't build a life being a poet. He was also friendly, witty, and obviously very gifted. When I saw that he was living with his wife and family in a Lower East Side slum, it hardly seemed to matter. When I noticed in a letter from him that the "K" key on his typewriter had no lower case, it was only an amusing distraction. Ted's apartment had marvelous paintings on the walls that were gifts from his friend Brainard, who would soon achieve relative affluence as a painter. Ted even had a gift from Andy Warhol: a painted wooden, three-dimensional, life-size Brillo Box.

I looked at the *romance* of his life, then, rather than at the harsh reality that lay under it, much as Ted himself seemed to do. We exchanged poems in the mail, each of us sending contributions to the other's literary magazine, and, in a limited way, we did some hanging out together. Ted and Ron once paid a visit to my East 45th Street apartment at a time when I was living briefly with a young woman named Jill, who happened to step into the apartment suddenly during their visit. Ted later told me he thought she looked like a heroine from a Godard film and that he instantly mentally recategorized me into the ranks of the great lovers. In effect, we each romanticized the other.

He published my poems in *C,* as I published the *C* gang's in the magazine I started that fall, *Lines.* We collaborated several times on poems, writing alternate lines on the typewriter at night in his brightly lit apartment. He favorably reviewed a chapbook of poems in which my work appeared with that of two other young poets. We gave a reading together. And he wrote an introduction to my first small collection.

But more than all of that, he let me see his life with his first wife, Sandy, and their two young children, David and Kate, in a way that comprised an implicit acceptance of me as a person — something, I realize now, even more important to me at the time than his literary approval. For all the bluster and bravado he could summon at certain moments, Ted was essentially a shy, deeply caring, most tenderhearted man. This unexpected glimpse of his own deeper self was offered so offhandedly that I only half-consciously recognized the personal generosity implicit in it.

He was, in this way, the least parochial of poets. He was an Irishman from a working-class family in Providence, a Korean veteran who had done his Master's thesis at Tulsa on George Bernard Shaw. I was an Armenian Jewish New Yorker — son of a famous writer — nine years his junior, who would seem to have shared so little of his background and allegiances that all but the most casual friendship would be a virtual impossibility. Yet somehow, during those first years on my own, Ted was a combination of friend and older brother, critic and collaborator, teacher and general interlocutor that made him perhaps the essential figure of my beginning as writer and adult, equally. And like his mentor, Frank O'Hara, he assumed at least as large a role in the lives of many others. His presence was like a warming sun at the center of the downtown literary life.

Years later, after getting married, moving to the West Coast, and becoming a family man myself, Ted was still an ideal reader at the back of my mind as I wrote. One of his memorably telling responses to a piece of writing was to mark it — in a soft, erasable pencil — A + , meaning the writer had given a marvelous performance, maybe just a bit too marvelous to be, after all, anything *more* than a performance. The style and substance of such a criticism was particularly salutary to a young poet in the first, heady flush of his powers. Ted could kid one out of an assumed portentousness faster and more painlessly than anyone else I knew — sometimes merely with laughter.

But as compelling as his presence had been to me, inevitably, over the years of not seeing him, I gradually all but forgot what he had meant to me. Then, in the fall of 1982, I called him long-distance about a line from a poem of his I had in mind to use as the epigraph for a piece I was writing. Three thousand miles away in New York City someone picked up the phone and said hello in a barely audible voice.

"Ted?"

"Yes." The voice was only slightly louder, and not particularly friendly.

"This is Aram Saroyan. I . . . "

"Who the fuck is Aram Saroyan?" he said in a slow grumble, and then I could hear his familiar, soft, bubbling laughter. "How are you, man?"

We talked that afternoon for about an hour, and I hung up the phone astonished and moved. "Why did you wait so long to call?" he asked at one point in the midst of a mutual torrent of reminiscences. It was a naked, lovely thing to say even as I felt bad for him saying it. And then, reaching into the mysterious heart of our friendship — we had been discussing, among other things, my book about my father, *Last Rites,* and a lunch the three of us had shared years before in New York — he said, "I'm in this with you for life, Aram."

So it was that, less than a year later, when I heard of his death of intestinal failure at forty-eight on a sweltering July 4th in New York City, I felt even more poignantly what he intimated. He gave me a large permission, both exhilarating and chastening, across the threshold of my chosen path. He let me see him on his own path — as it turned out, all the way through. The relationship was real, troubling, finite, and beyond any measure I know. He was a great, surprising gift in my life, Ted Berrigan, and I won't be likely to forget that again.

3

During the spring of 1965, after I'd put out several issues of *Lines,* I got a letter from a young American poet named Tom Clark, who was doing graduate work in England and at the same time acting as poetry editor of *The Paris Review.* Clark mentioned seeing *Lines* and inquired politely about exchanging copies of our respective magazines, as well as asking for news of the New York poetry scene. *The Paris Review* was, of course, a major literary magazine and I instantly wrote him to set up the exchange and tried to tell him as best I could about the scene in New York.

If Ron Padgett was a disarmingly affable avant-gardist
and Ted Berrigan a sort of presiding spirit over the current
poetry scene in New York, I knew Tom Clark (from his
debut in Henry Rago's *Poetry*) to be the archetypal young
poet of my generation. By this I mean that his debut poems
in *Poetry* were dazzling achievements in approximately the
same tradition as I had taken up, in essence the Black
Mountain School. But I had found none of my own awk-
wardness in Clark's initial work; it seemed to me already
boldly comprehensive, not only in technique but in the life
it described, too. Crucially, there was a woman in his
poetry, referred to with just the right casual note. He
seemed to have it all, and I was jealous and suspicious as
well as admiring. In a few months' time, Tom was publishing in *The Paris Review* poems by Ron and Ted and me, as
well as others in the New York scene for whom we provided addresses, and had himself become a part of the
central axis of our scene.

My correspondence with Tom over the next couple of
years is extensive, since, more often than the others, he
wasn't available in person. Looking at examples of both
sides of this correspondence recently in the Special Collections Library at UCLA, I discovered two young men at the
beginning of their adult lives, dedicated to becoming writers yet, between the details of publishing and writing,
occasionally betraying loneliness and confusion and un-
steadiness in their common pursuit. During the late summer of 1966, when I went to London for two months,
Tom, who lived a train ride away in Essex, was the first
person with whom I got in touch. When we met in a
restaurant in Chelsea, I encountered a tall, handsome
young man who seemed slightly ragged with the details of
his day and spoke with the clear, open-voweled accent of
the Midwest. We were sitting in the back of a hamburger
place and had hit on Ezra Pound as a topic. Tom was telling

Tom Clark in the backyard of his home, Bolinas,
California, 1972. Photo © by Gerard Malanga.

me everything he could think of about him. I was only half
interested but delighted to meet him. Like Ted Berrigan,
but without his easy social command, Tom liked to pop
pills and talk, or rather, as the word was just then, rap.

Going over our correspondence in the locked room
with the buzzer door at the UCLA Special Collections Library the other day was a little unnerving. Here were, quite
literally, the pages of our youth — mixed up, shook up, and
on my side frequently obtuse — had somehow gotten

themselves inside a vaulted institution for the purpose of study by scholars.

I remember visiting Tom in his apartment in a tract house in Essex where he was a teaching fellow and, after sharing one of innumerable hashish cigarettes, both of us huddling rapt over his little portable monaural phonograph and listening to "Zip-a-dee-doo-da" by Bob E. Sox, a treasured Motown single from his record collection. As he eloquently describes in *Late Returns,* his memoir of Ted Berrigan, he was just then trying to shed the academic emphasis of his poetry background at the University of Michigan (where, like Frank O'Hara, he had won a Hopwood Award) and pick up on the new American sound he had discerned in Berrigan, Padgett, and others. I had become, by this time, a dedicated minimalist, the author of such one-word poems as "lighght," and liked to affect an impatience with anything less radical. But at bottom we were two young men at the moment without girlfriends who were partaking of the chemical and herbal options of the period with compensatory fervor.

I was fond of speaking messianically of "the new consciousness." Tom could grow bored or intimidated enough by this to affect a country-bumpkin-like obtusity and giggle or taunt me back with the phrase. 1966 may indeed have been, in certain quarters, an epoch of new consciousness, but when I remember an overnight at Tom's in Essex that summer it now seems a more or less classic story of bachelor quarters with the concomitant small irritations.

4

That fall, back in America again, I moved into a two-story row house on Watson Street off of Central Square in Cambridge, Massachusetts. Over the course of the next year I

Clark Coolidge, 1976. Photo © by Gerard
Malanga.

shared the house with several others. Most significantly, in
a couple of months' time, Clark Coolidge, a poet from
Providence, moved in and we commenced a daily dialogue
on the direction our work was taking.

Clark was twenty-seven or so and coming off of a divorce and very likely was more upset about it than I had
any way of fathoming. He was a former jazz drummer (his
father was the retired chairman of the Music Department
at Brown) who had read Kerouac and dropped out of
college and eventually began writing poetry that had

something of the quick synaptic changes of jazz and Kerouac combined. While still in New York I had published
his first collection, *Flag Flutter & U.S. Electric,* as a Lines
book (I had discontinued the magazine in the fall of 1965
after six issues) and his poems had created a stir of excite-
ment among Ted, Ron, Tom, and others in what is loosely
referred to as the New York School.

Clark was a tall, affable, Clark Kent look-alike who had
a kind of steadiness of manner that made it possible for us
to share quarters without major upheavals. There were
usually one or two others also sharing the house, and I
became the self-elected dishwasher of the place. It seemed
to be therapeutic and, needless to say, no one was racing me
to the sink.

He and I sometimes had arguments about our work—I
seem to have wanted him to be more minimal, as if poetry
were an argument you could win. I was still a very young
man, very uncertain of my terms. Clark, on the other hand,
was generally a strong supporter of my work, and living in
a household in which a literary dialogue was in progress
made it easier for me to make a significant decision.

The previous winter in Hollywood—having been
flown out there first-class from New York courtesy of
Twentieth Century-Fox—I had read for Mike Nichols for
the title role in *The Graduate.* Nichols had liked my reading
and asked me to do a screen test. Then there had been a long
delay and it wasn't until I'd been in the Watson Street
household for several months that I got the call from Hollywood to come out to test. By that time, I'd decided to say
no. I was a writer, not an actor.

I won't pretend that in the years since that phone call I
haven't had moments of doubt, wondering whether I
hadn't made a big mistake. But these have been only moments and, in fact, I've never seriously regretted the decision that gave me the life I've chosen, as opposed to the

very real possibility of having a high-powered life *handed* to me based on no particular effort of my own.

In the first place, I knew too many hardworking young actors—including the young Robert De Niro—who would have died and gone to heaven to get such a role. It seemed absurd for a non-actor like myself, who had no particular interest in the craft, to be given such a plum. I was told by friends that I looked the role, and wouldn't have to know how to act, but at the beginning of my adulthood I needed more than anything else, it seemed, to assert my own goals, my own will power. There is a line in Camus to the effect that the man who says no says yes, which I take to mean that an assertion of will, of choice, even if it is negative, represents an affirmation of values. When I saw the movie a year or so later I was sitting beside my future wife, Gailyn McClanahan, and if over the years I've had moments of doubting my choice, these have been quickly dispelled by the realization that, had I in the end gotten the part, I never would have met her. Watching the movie, it was also clear that Dustin Hoffman, an actor who had toiled for years for an opportunity like *The Graduate,* gave a masterful performance I could never have matched. Finally, there may have been an element in the sixties themselves that gave me support for the decision I made.

5

By the early summer of 1967 Clark had moved out of the Watson Street house and gone to San Francisco, where he became the drummer in David and Tina Meltzer's rock group, The Serpent Power. Not long after Clark left, Tom (who had come back from England to settle into an apartment on East Fourteenth Street in Manhattan) and Ron and Ted all drove up to Cambridge together for a visit of

several days. The weather was lovely and we figured out
makeshift sleeping arrangements in the house for the three
of them and then paired off variously or sometimes wan-
dered off alone, enjoying a moment that in retrospect was
probably the sixties at its innocent height. The Beatles'
album *Sergeant Pepper's Lonely Hearts Club Band* had just
come out and on many Cambridge streets it could be heard
on the sidewalk through the open windows of households
of our contemporaries.

After several days of wandering Harvard Square, listening to *Sergeant Pepper* on various stereos, talking about
poetry, smoking grass, and watching the girls go by in
their miniskirts, Ron and Tom took off back to New York
while Ted invited me to come along to Lowell, Massachusetts, where he was going to interview Jack Kerouac for
The Paris Review. A poet I hadn't met before named Duncan
McNaughton had also been enlisted, and when he arrived
in his car the three of us immediately took off in it for
Lowell.

For me, meeting Kerouac proved to be a kind of literary
baptism, a completely unexpected one because I imagined
the sixties had long since delivered me beyond any such
old-fashioned sacrament. I'm talking about the era of acid,
when for five dollars you could experience a full day of a
state of mind that had been compared to Buddhist enlight-
enment. I had seen the light more than once by now and
was sure Jack Kerouac would be little more than a quaint
literary curiosity. I came along because Ted, knowing that
Kerouac had loved my father's work, thought he might be
more responsive in an interview with me in tow.

The other day at UCLA I came across a letter I had
written Tom Clark in England from my apartment on
West 85th Street just a year or so before this visit, in which
I spoke about how much I loved Kerouac's work, which I
was reading just then stoned on marijuana. Perhaps it says

Jack Kerouac and his wife, Stella. 1968. Photo by
James Coyne. Courtesy of Allen Ginsberg.

something about the chemistry of the period that by the
time of the interview I seemed to have forgotten the keen
pleasure I had taken in *Desolation Angels,* for instance,
among other books by Kerouac.

No matter; I dare say Jack Kerouac was more than even
Ted, who never questioned his genius and knew his work
comprehensively, had bargained for. The interview,
unique in *The Paris Review's* Art of Fiction series, is one of
Ted's (and Jack's) masterpieces and may be savored in its
entirety in the magazine or the book in which it's reprinted.
What I saw was a man who, nearing the end of his life (in
1969 at the age of forty-seven), was disillusioned with his

spiritual offspring, the sixties generation that would seem
to have taken to heart his and the rest of the Beat Generation's leads. But he told us angrily he could get a heart
attack from LSD and defended an older America of purpose
and ambition and men walking swiftly through the streets.
He preferred his old Horace Mann classmate William F.
Buckley, Jr. to Abbie Hoffman or Jerry Rubin. And somewhere along the line, through loud outbursts and com-
ically obscene exclamations, through transparent personal
despair and equally transparent defiance, it came to me that
I was in the presence of a human marvel, a genius of human
nakedness, so to speak, who could, even in the advanced
state of ruin in which we found him, still teach us something about what a man really was, and about what really
mattered in life. I knew Kerouac was "wrong" in most of
what he said — although, of course, he was right about
most everything — but at the same time I saw that he was
being more boldly open with three strangers from another
and a younger generation — three emissaries from the sup-
posedly liberated, enlightened sixties generation — than
we were in the habit of being with one another.

6

A few weeks later during that summer of 1967, the fabled
"Summer of Love," a book of my minimal poetry was
accepted by Random House; and on the day I went down
to New York to meet my editor there, Christopher Cerf, I
met my future wife, Gailyn, who was staying at the house
of the friend from whom I was getting the ride to New
York. I can still see her as I first saw her. Blond and beautiful, she stood framed in a doorway in the morning sunlight
wearing a sleeveless flower print dress, and it seemed to me
that she was very brave to be so lightly attired, so seem-

ingly unencumbered, inside the big roaring world just then. She had just graduated from Goucher College in Baltimore. Sharing with her the back seat of our mutual friend's VW on the drive down to New York, I learned that we had in common the same minimal-conceptual taste in the arts. She was the first person I met outside of the poetry scene who knew and liked the work of the sculptor Donald Judd, for instance, with its rows of identical metal boxes.

That fall, by now living with Gailyn in an apartment on River Street in Cambridge, I stopped writing poetry — having carried my minimalist aesthetic as far as I could — and didn't take it up again with any real energy for another five years. A few months later I began to phase out marijuana. The following spring in New York, Tom Clark got married, and Clark Coolidge married again during the same period. With the finding of our mates, a new era was inaugurated. When I started to write again, in the late summer of 1972 in Bolinas, California, it wasn't minimal poetry anymore, but a long poem about my life, marriage, and fatherhood. Strawberry Saroyan had been born at the hospital in Stoneham, Massachusetts on October 20, 1970, which is probably the most accurate date I could give for the end of *my* sixties.

7

The most disturbing thing about the written commemorations of the sixties I've seen — and new ones seem to arrive almost weekly at the local library — is that they dwell without exception on the political side of the period. *The Sixties: Years of Hope, Days of Rage; 1968; Chicago 1968,* and so forth. And yet, as the foregoing indicates, my own and most of my friends' sixties experience were all but apolitical, the single paramount exception being a concern to avoid the draft. What bothers me most about the political emphasis per se is that it skirts what remains the period's deepest and most protean element, which, while not explicitly political, was surely its more revolutionary aspect too. The sixties was about happiness.

One remembers that even at the time this was the reality least likely to be reported, perhaps because it didn't lend itself to any established genre of journalism. Indeed, the primary literary mode of my generation is poetry and during the late sixties and early seventies numerous anthologies of this work were published (a number of them going into multiple printings). Where are the poets who seemed most representative of that time today? They are in many different places but you are not likely to find them in the current anthologies. And this at the same moment we are told there is a revival of the period in progress in fashion, music, and movies, as well as books. One wonders what exactly the revival comprises. A commercial opportunity, perhaps—but one orchestrated to avoid the period's deeper and more potent dynamics?

At the Woodstock Rock Festival in 1969 Abbie Hoffman was kicked off the stage by Pete Townsend of The Who when Hoffman attempted to politicize the proceedings. Here is a clear registration of the apolitical tenor of much that went on. Yet only a year or two later Townsend apologized publicly to Hoffman in his *Rolling Stone* interview and said that if asked now, he'd be happy to play a political benefit. This may have been one of the first suggestions of what evolved into the Music Aid benefits that took off during the eighties, surely one of the important legacies of the spirit, if not the letter, of the period. In effect, these events represent a powerful realization of that model of the communal in the personal, and the political in the communal, that existed in nascent form during the sixties.

Sixties into
Seventies

Gailyn & Aram Saroyan, St. Mark's Church, New York City 1969. Photo by Jayne Nodland.

I

In the spring of 1969, Gailyn and I went up to Woodstock, New York, from Manhattan, hoping to find a place to live for a while outside the pressures of the city. My second book of poems with Random House, *Pages,* was about to come out and I was in the midst of that uneasy sensation young writers know when they first begin to show their face to the world.

I remember that spring in color, maybe because we were in Woodstock, and possibly too because of Bob Dylan's blue cover on *Nashville Skyline,* an album that came out within the first few days we were there. We were over at Mason Hoffenberg's house one morning and he had bought a copy of it, or maybe Dylan had brought him over a copy, and he put it on and I instantly loved it. Dylan's voice seemed to be coming from deep inside him, and he sounded like a happy man.

At that time Gailyn and I were beginning to let our hair down with each other, and with me that period was also marked with literally long hair, as well as purple shirt, blue bellbottoms, and dark brown suede jacket. We had been eating fairly strictly macrobiotically for a few months and it felt good walking on country roads.

One afternoon we walked into the Colonial Drugstore in the little shopping plaza on the main street of town to ask the proprietor about a property he rented. It turned out the place wasn't available, and while listening to the man I turned to my right to meet the eyes of someone who had stepped up to the counter to make a purchase. The eyes were casual. It was Bob Dylan. The druggist, an elderly man, greeted him with a sprightly "Hi!" and Dylan placed an order with him for something I didn't quite catch.

"Box or case?" the druggist asked.

Dylan lingered lightly over the question and then sig-
naled "case" as if giving way to the easiest solution. There
was a lovely modesty in the way he did this.

All this happened quickly in the corner of my eye as
Gailyn and I made our way out of the store. She was
wearing a Persian dress with tiny mirrors sewn into it, and
yellow silk pants. When we were outside the store, I turned
to her and said, "Guess who that guy was at the counter?"

"Who?" she asked.

"Bob Dylan."

"You're kidding?"

"No, I really should introduce myself, or say hi, or something."

"Sure."

I turned around. We were nearly to the edge of the
shopping plaza's parking lot, and Dylan was just coming
out of the drugstore. I began walking toward him and as he
reached the door of his car—a wood-paneled ranch wagon—I called to him.

"Hey, Bob?"

Dylan was a vision in tan. His (now short) hair, the color
of his face, his shirt, pants, and shoes, were all varieties of
that hue. He didn't respond particularly to my call but
continued with a kind of steady deliberation about the
business of opening the door of his station wagon and
getting in beside one of his children in the front seat.

I wasn't sure whether or not he would start his car and
pull away, but I didn't run—that would have violated
whatever feeling I was taking to him. He didn't start the
motor. He waited staring approximately at the steering
wheel as I jogged the last few steps and bent down by the
window.

"Bob," I said, "I'm Aram Saroyan. I sent you a book last
spring—did you ever get it?"

Dylan didn't look up. He seemed to be breathing very deeply. After some time he said, "I don't believe so." His voice was a great deal deeper than I expected, and his speaking rhythm had the slow deliberation of a much older man.

"It was a Random House book," I told him, "with a black and white cover?"

After another considered pause, he said, "I don't believe I got it." He still hadn't looked at me.

My mind was racing, and it was as though Dylan was putting pressure on it from another direction. I couldn't think of anything more to say and moved my head up from his window.

Then I remembered. "Well," I said with the hesitation of a new momentum, "I just heard your new album. It's really beautiful."

The scene began to change. Dylan for the first time raised his head, as my own had receded, and then he looked at me.

"Oh, I'm so glad you like it," he told me with the tenor of clear sincerity.

I was in the midst of a chemical reorientation and nodded and said, "It's beautiful, it really is," while at the same time turning away, back toward Gailyn, who had waited for me near the edge of the parking lot.

2

We weren't able to find a place for rent and, after staying for five weeks at a motel that had a room with a kitchenette and a television for forty dollars a week, we went back to New York City. I had very little money and it was going to be impossible for us to continue renting anywhere. The bottom was falling out of our lives, but we were eating so well and feeling so good it didn't seem to matter. It's interesting to have things fall through sometimes because after a while you notice your heart continues to beat, things continue to go on, but on another level, and not necessarily a worse one.

Virginia Admiral, our old friend, offered us free lodging in her loft on West Broadway while it was being remodeled so she could rent out the front half of it. Gailyn bought a two-burner hot-plate and cooked beautiful meals of brown rice with almonds, sauteed vegetables, and beans. Often we had fish too. The loft was large and empty and each morning at around eight an Irish carpenter named McDaid came through a hole in the wall and began working. There was a toilet but no shower or bath, but Virginia had a full bathroom at her business, Academy Typing Service, which we used whenever we needed. The loft was on the top floor, the fifth, and looking back — despite its inconveniences, or maybe because of them — it was the most satisfying place I ever lived in the city.

We stayed there for five months, through the summer. New York in the summertime has always been a peculiarly exhilarating experience to me, perhaps because the heat is so much a force to contend with that the passage of time is a small triumph by itself. I loved walking with Gailyn at night — the air was almost liquid, and the Village was always teeming with eager tourists of all varieties. I had nothing in mind for once, and allowed myself that luxury without trying too hard to see what lay on the other side of it.

I remember the loft at night, the wood floor under the bare bulb that was our sole light source in the dark. We had been together for two years and during that time had rid ourselves of most of our possessions. We had met and lived for six months together in Brookline and Cambridge, Massachusetts; gone to Paris for a few weeks; lived for ten months in New York attending sessions with a psychiatrist singly, jointly, and at separate group therapies; then we'd gone to Berkeley for three months; then back to New York; Woodstock; and now we were going through the summer in Manhattan as not unhappy paupers. When the small amount of our belongings we had put into storage in Berkeley arrived back in New York, I sold them to Virginia for the price of the mover's bill. She got a bed, a KLH stereo radio-phonograph, and a color TV for her loft, and we were able to use them there for the interim before she moved in.

We had the big double bed in the middle of the room, and at the foot of it there was a long low table across which was arranged the KLH, the television, and the hotplate. It was the summer of the moon landing — a strangely lame feat. But one night there was a television program of Joni Mitchell singing her songs, and when she sang "For Free" I found myself crying. I'm still not sure why, most likely a combination of things, including her resemblance to Gailyn and a song about doing something without making money. My second book of poems was out and I wasn't making money, but it was great to cry about anything. I hadn't for so long.

3

That fall we had to go on, had to move — the energy was there and wouldn't be denied — and so we took off on a Greyhound across America.

In San Francisco we stayed for a few days with my Aunt Cosette, my father's sister, a woman of seventy who was always exceptionally kind to us. We then took a bus up to Mendocino to look into the commune scene, very big that year. We visited several, but none was very inviting. These places seemed to be either authority structures for people seeking that, or anarchies that weren't quite working out.

One place we visited was only half built, with the rainy season threatening. It was a depressing scene we left without saying goodbye, having sensed our own intrusion.

We were hitching down the coast, back to San Francisco, when we were left off at an intersection where a young man sat on a railing beside the Navarre River. This young guy had a stray eye, and because of it, a slightly sinister aspect, but I forged ahead with a wave hello. Then, when the three of us proceeded onto the back of a pickup that had stopped for us, he invited us to his campsite just down the road, offering us nuts and raisins.

We had to accept. It was the end of the day, darkening, and it was what we had come out here for in the first place. The camp proved to be a lovely scene, with a roaring fire and a mixture of couples and single people, and we were given a sleeping bag by our friend. As night came on, we sat listening to songs (one guy sang Dylan's "Just Like Tom Thumb Blues," which I knew too), and we were given a delicious cup of soup, cooked over the open fire by a guy with a Finnish accent. A gregarious European spirit among the spaced-out Americans.

We were on the verge of begging admittance to the camp for a longer stay when something put us off. Some people who had left to get beer arrived after a delay due to an accident at the intersection where we'd met our friend. I began to feel that however lovely the camp and the surroundings, as well as the people, things were still dangerously spaced-out. We would go on in the morning, we decided, which we did. But that night gave us our first taste of the outdoors—we slept under the trees and the stars with the camp dogs and other bodies close by.

4

When we got back to New York that fall, we started going through a series of changes that eventually led to our having our first child, Strawberry. It started on the trip back, actually, when we visited our friend Sandy Berrigan, who had a house at the time in Iowa City. Our last night there we split a tab of acid and went on a visit to some neighbors who had two children, one still a baby.

Back in New York on the Lower East Side, we started going about the business of refilling Gailyn's prescription for birth control pills and let a little snag in the process be our signal to forget it — and have a baby. I was twenty-six, Gailyn was twenty-four — why wait any longer for our life to begin, the money would figure itself out.

We stayed in New York's crazed Albert Hotel for a few weeks, in a tiny room with no view, no ventilation, but a kitchenette that allowed us to get back on our diet. Then a while at my grandmother's on Park Avenue, an exercise in self-annihilation that even so may have been the scene of our conception bed. Journeyed on to Washington, DC for six uneasy weeks at the Georgetown townhouse of Gailyn's parents, Grant and Pauli. As we were leaving, Gailyn got tentative word she was pregnant.

After we left Georgetown, we went back up to New York, and then found our way to the little town of Marblehead, just north of Boston. By now, I had cut my hair. We stayed for a while in a guest house and then moved into an apartment in the remodeled upstairs of a widow's house, a kindly old lady named Hazel Chichette.

Marblehead was our first small-town experience, but we knew almost no one there and got to know very few people before we left. It is a picture-postcard New England town — I once had the sensation that everything in it was slightly smaller than the real thing, akin to the feeling I had at the Grand Canyon that I was looking at the *real* photograph of the place. Our daily regimen involved a mile or so walk to the library, where we perhaps checked out a book or two, and the same walk back. The trees were beautiful there—it was April when we arrived and we stayed through the brilliant fall into December—and the birdsong was ecstatic.

5

We arrived in Marblehead in the spring of 1970 as a couple (though Gailyn was growing) and left it in the winter of that year as a family of three. We had gone through a natural childbirth experience at the hospital in Stoneham, that was perfect in every way except for the doctor's last-minute suggestion of an episiotomy, which, had we waited a few more minutes for the vulva to dilate and grow numb, would have been entirely unnecessary. The cut was slow to heal and Gailyn could feel it months afterwards.

But even with an episiotomy Gailyn had triumphed— she'd taken herself through all the stages of the labor without any significant pain and she had had no anesthetic up to the last-minute episiotomy. We left Marblehead with a stretch of seven months behind us in which we'd faced a new experience with energy and consistency and we felt good.

At the last minute Gailyn had had to switch doctors and hospitals because her original doctor had decided the baby was late, and that if nothing happened in the next week he'd have to induce labor. He seemed to be put off by Gailyn's attitude: she approached the experience joyfully and he seemed to want moans and groans. I talked with him on the phone and tried to get him to reverse his decision but he wouldn't hear of it. Then he talked with Gailyn and started saying things like "This baby may die!" With that, we moved quickly to find another doctor and hospital, and that very night Gailyn got her labor. Even at the enlightened Stoneham hospital, there was — in addition to the episiotomy — the imbecility of shaving the pubic hair. Why? Would it get in the way?

We left Marblehead when Strawberry was only six weeks old and went down to Manhattan, where we stayed for a month in my sister Lucy's apartment, a one-room palace, while she was out of town. Then we flew to LA, where we stayed for six weeks in my mother and stepfather's guest house. During this visit, we experienced the great earthquake of 1971.

I was dreaming about waking up in a used car in a used-car lot and having to convince the proprietor of the lot that I knew how to drive (I hadn't learned yet). I woke up and the room was rocking back and forth like a washing machine. I turned to Gailyn and asked, "What is it?" She said, "It's an earthquake." Always has her wits about her, this woman. What I might have had in mind, God only knows.

After our six weeks there, we took a train back across the country, with stops along the way in Albuquerque, Sante Fe, and Chicago. On the last stretch of our ride, in the middle of the night before we arrived in New York, I woke up in the top berth above Gailyn and Strawberry, having dreamed a particularly vivid dream of flying.

Back in New York, we checked into the Chelsea Hotel, and I went about various possible projects to deliver us out of our impending poverty. One of these was an idea for a show that I suggested to a big Amsterdam museum while I was calling them long-distance regarding another matter (some posters of one-word poems they were interested in

buying). An empty museum. I told them I would appear in
person to handle the resounding tremors that would be felt
throughout the art world when the show opened. No such
luck. Among other things, the museum didn't know
where to put all their art during the show.

Finally we had to get out of the Chelsea — it's so expensive there. My stepfather lent me $500 (which I still owe
him) and we went up to Cambridge and found a little
second-floor apartment at 2 Belvedere Place. It was April
and the apartment looked pretty and we were exhausted.

6

A year later, on April 1, 1972, we moved out of our apartment and drove to the western part of the state to the Log
Cabin Motel in Goshen. We took up residence here to look
around the area for a permanent place to live in the country.
We were a little north of the Berkshires, quite high up, and
there was still snow on the ground.

Our cabin at the motel had a front living room area with
a kitchenette, and in the back was a small bedroom. The
rooms had a funny smell I thought had something to do
with the plastic, pseudo-country style furnishings. A short
time after we arrived, I developed a severe headache. I also
misplaced the front door key and had to go to the proprietor's house across the parking lot to get another one.
The combination of the misplaced key — we told ourselves
Strawberry, one and a half years old now, had done something with it — and the inexplicable headache (I hadn't had
one so bad in years) gave a surreal quality to our first night
there.

I had a job teaching at two schools in Massachusetts. I
was designated a "Poet-in-the-Schools," a part of the National Endowment for the Arts teaching program. My job

was to conduct two classes each week at each of the two schools, one a class for students and the other a class for teachers. One school was in Worcester, in just about the middle of Massachusetts, and the other in Brookline, next to Boston, all the way across the state from Goshen. We had moved out of Cambridge before the program ended for the summer because we were terribly crowded and guilty and on edge in the apartment, which had light and a nice view but had grown too small for us. When we'd moved in, exactly a year to the day before we left, Strawberry had been a baby. While we were there she learned to walk and the apartment shrank. In addition, we were on the middle floor in a three-story building, sandwiched between a young single woman upstairs and a Harvard sophomore below us equipped with a stereo that made the floor tremble.

Both were agreeable enough people, the Harvard sophomore always willing to turn the volume down, but we were embarrassed to have to ask this when we often had nightly spells of crying from our child and there were no complaints about this. Also, having a child in a city is a frustrating experience on a number of other counts. There is no place for casual play — if she falls down on the sidewalk she hurts herself. In Cambridge the air pollution during the winter reached frightening levels — at night sometimes the air seemed to be some sort of gas. I learned this was a consequence of having a taxi lot within a block of us. The drivers left their engines on to keep warm while they waited for calls, and the neighborhood — in a sort of valley below Massachusetts Avenue — filled up with fumes. I complained about the air to municipal authorities, but it wasn't an easy thing to control.

7

From the Log Cabin Motel, I drove to Worcester to begin the week and "taught" a class of third-graders how to write poetry. The class genius was a handsome young fellow named Dan, who had embarked on an ongoing epic based on his name: "I am Dan/I eat out of a can/I am Dan/I use Dry Ban/I am Dan/When I go to the beach I get a tan." He had close to a hundred verses and the accumulation was nothing short of powerful. On this particular day — one of my final sessions with the class — I asked for suggestions for a title for the magazine of their work we were preparing to mimeograph. I had written various suggestions on the board when Dan's hand shot up and I called on him.

"Imagination on Paper," he drawled out, and a few minutes later this title won by a landslide.

The next day — we were planning to work on finding a place after I finished my teaching on the first three days of each week — I drove to Worcester again to teach a class of teachers. This experience was mainly an exercise in restraint — there was such a variety of sincere but limited interest. The class was almost entirely made up of women. After I had brought up most of the information I had to offer in the first few classes, it mainly became a sort of extended conversation about various poems, including children's work from their own classes.

After I arrived back in Goshen, we had dinner and then took a drive into Northampton and visited friends there. Arriving back at our cabin in the dark and cold, we reencountered the peculiar odor with renewed wariness. The room had a gas heater that was thermostatically controlled, but I had dismissed the idea that the smell was gas when we originally moved in. It smelled more like plastic.

The next morning I had to drive to Brookline and I woke early, eager to get a good start on the long drive. I had a few swallows of hot tea, then kissed Gailyn, still in bed half-asleep, goodbye. I had a curiously absent feeling as I drove to the highway, and somehow couldn't remember the way, though I'd taken the same route the past couple of days. After driving some fifteen or twenty miles, I realized I'd taken a ten-mile detour, turned around, made my way back, and finally got onto the freeway.

I was planning to have breakfast at a Howard Johnson's along the way, but was eager to make up for the time I'd lost and decided to drive for a while longer before stopping to eat. I passed two women standing beside their stalled car by the side of the highway, and felt a self-satisfied sense of security within my moving vehicle — a 1967 Renault I'd bought shortly after learning to drive in Cambridge (and then had to learn to drive all over again because it was standard shift). The car hadn't been perfect — I'd spent money almost weekly maintaining it — but here it was running, and there were those two women by the side of the road. As the warm glow of security and mobility spread over me — though tinged with guilt at not stopping to help the women, however clear it was I couldn't afford the time — I began to neaten the maps in the glove compartment, which was just below the steering wheel in this car.

Then I heard a noise. When I looked up I saw the car had gone off the road and was headed for an embankment. It was too late for me to do anything but turn the wheel as far as I could back toward the road. In the next instant the car crashed into the snow-covered embankment. The windshield — shattered in a thousand pieces but frozen in its frame — had detached itself from the car. The right front tire had come through the floorboard to the right passenger seat. I noticed the rearview mirror was tilted in a vertical, instead of horizontal, position. I sat for a moment before gathering the energy to get out.

Miraculously I was unscratched, but my life had been irrevocably changed. We left Massachusetts the next day in a rented car and drove to the house of friends in Philadelphia. From there, with friends we went to New York and then took a plane to London. From London, Gailyn, Strawberry and I made our way to Bolinas, California. All this took place during the three months following the accident, which had happened in the blink of an eye. Later that morning, I called Gailyn at the motel to let her know what had happened. Having been puzzled that she and Strawberry were finding it harder and harder to get up each morning, she had just realized we were all getting progressively gassed by the faulty thermostatic heater.

We were lucky to be alive, and it was almost as if we'd gone out of one lifetime and into another.

8

We arrived in Bolinas in July of 1972 and lucked out to find a house to rent on the mesa. I began to notice the moon, its phases, for the first time in my life. Gailyn made a quilt, a beautiful blending of the colors of dawn and twilight. I wrote my first novel, about New York, which I got nostalgic for in the middle of our first winter in the country. Strawberry learned to talk.

Friends of ours got us into the town and then left us on our own. It is a small town, where identities would merge and blur in the ebb and flow of feelings. We did things to keep ourselves there. We let ourselves have another baby. As the time approached we gradually decided to have it by ourselves, without even a midwife in attendance. Our neighbors, Carmen and Richie Quinones, who were from New York and had five children of their own, were across the street in case anything went wrong. They had taken part in several home deliveries.

When Cream was out, lying tiny beside Gailyn in the wood-paneled living room only a little after dark on November 26, 1973, I ran across the street to tell them, and Carmen told me how to cut the cord. "Tie it tight," she said, and I did. We all got seriously sick for the first time just after we moved onto the mesa—staph infection. Gailyn and Strawberry got it first, and then I got it a couple of months later. One night, coming home from a day in San Francisco, as I walked from the bus stop on Main Street up to the mesa, I felt my body go dead, exhausted. That night in the mirror I could see the white spots on my gums that were our particular variety of infection—trench mouth.

I cured myself with rest and vitamins, while Gailyn took over building the fires for two weeks of the wettest, coldest winter in years (the winter the eucalyptus trees died, or almost died.)

My mother and stepfather came out to visit us one afternoon and my eleven-year-old half-brother, Charlie, wanted to know what I did with myself all day. Mostly I was writing. After ten years of cleaning the gun, I let it do some hunting.

One summer evening I went out the back door and stood in our driveway and surveyed the hush at the end of the day just before the light failed. I breathed in the fragrance of Bolinas, looked over at the fence I had made, and my gaze fell smack onto Richie's on the other side of the fence in the middle of his own reverie.

We stayed in Bolinas, eventually in a house of our own, for twelve years, the longest either Gailyn or I had lived anywhere in our lives.

Friends in
the World

(Left to right) Victor Bockris, Aram Saroyan, Andrew Wylie.
London, 1972.

I

Part of the real luck of one's life, I think, is in one's friends. And just what the personal alchemy is that, at any given moment, strikes a chord between two people is mysterious, involving more than the capacity of two people to enjoy each other's company. There is an element of timing that may, at a certain moment, galvanize a friendship and, later on, let it languish.

I first saw Andrew Wylie one night in Casey's Restaurant in Harvard Square in the fall of 1966. I was sitting in a booth having a hamburger and talking with a young man named Eugene Pool, whom I never saw again after that evening. I'd recently moved to a house in Central Square in Cambridge, having given up an apartment in New York City the previous August and gone to London for two months. I liked the human scale of Cambridge after New York's relentless war on the nerves, but I knew very few people there. Eugene Pool had written an article about my concrete-minimalist poetry for the *Boston Globe*'s Sunday magazine section and we were meeting now, more or less in friendly formality, for me to thank him for the generous praise he'd given my work. Our booth happened to be close to the entrance of Casey's, and toward the end of the meal Pool looked up — he sat facing the inside of the restaurant while I faced the entrance — and nodded at somebody leaving and then said hello. By the time I looked to the side of our table, Andrew Wylie was standing there with his wife Christina.

They were the most radiantly handsome couple I'd ever seen. I thought they looked like Percy and Mary Shelley must have looked, not so much in their exact faces and coloring, because Andrew and Christina were both fair-haired — Andrew red-headed, Christina a blond — but in the luminous quality they both possessed, in their radiance. I had no idea who they were, but wished right away that I knew them and envied Pool that he did. They all said hello, there was a quick introduction, and I said hello to them too, and then they went away. After they left I asked Pool about them, and he spoke, as I remember, only about Andrew, telling me he was "brilliant," an undergraduate at Harvard, and a poet.

After that evening I kept an eye out for Wylie when I was in Harvard Square and it was a month or two later that I sat opposite him in a booth in the Parnassus restaurant one midday. He was sitting next to a writer named Bill Ferguson who had started a small press in Cambridge. I didn't like Ferguson's agenda for his press, mainly because it didn't include me or any of the writers I felt close to, and in those days of my early twenties I alternated between a very brash come-on socially and an extreme introspection in which I felt semi-invisible. In fact I was a shy out-of-towner, but I was also very arrogant about my work and the work of my New York School contemporaries. I thought Ferguson was being stodgy and I was impatient to make a connection in the scene, a connection I quickly realized wasn't about to happen. As I gave up hope, I told him he was publishing boring work and had missed out on a very exciting scene. I was waiting for Wylie to tip his hand one way or the other, hoping for an ally of course, but he didn't say anything at all.

2

I didn't see him again after that for another four and a half years. I'd left Cambridge, published two books of poetry, gotten married, and become a father. Then in April of 1971

Gailyn and I and Strawberry, our half-a-year old daughter, moved into a small, light-filled, second floor apartment in a three-story building on Belvedere Place between Harvard and Central Squares. The Cambridge folksinger Paul Geremia told me that the blues singer Taj Mahal had once had the same apartment in the same building and that his mail-box name-plate had read, with a becoming modesty, "T. Mahal."

Not long after we'd settled into the apartment I was walking along Massachusetts Avenue opposite Harvard Yard one bright spring morning when I saw a young man wheeling a baby carriage down the street at a speed that seemed hazardous. The young man was beginning to go thin on top and wore a white shirt opened at the collar, dark slacks, and oxfords. And he was smoking a cigarette, taking puff after puff as he directed the baby carriage one-handed, as if his speed was a function of the smoke he was generating. I moved over on the sidewalk to give him the wide berth he needed, and it wasn't till after he'd passed that it came to me dimly that I knew the young man, that it was that fellow Wylie I'd met years before. As a father myself now, I was both amused and reassured to see him dealing with the demands of the same situation I knew in so transparently harried a manner. Being suddenly a family man had knocked the wind out of me, too, though I tried to hide it.

Not long after this, Wylie asked me to read at a big group reading he was organizing as a benefit for the Red Book, a socialist bookstore in Central Square. I remember standing on the corner of Plympton Street and Massachusetts Avenue, just up from Gordon Cairnie's Grolier Bookshop, with Wylie and the poet John Weiners on another bright morning as Weiners passed out leaflets to passersby. I've forgotten what the leaflet was about, perhaps the announcement of the opening of a new restaurant. John's

state of mind during this period was precarious: he seemed
to be drifting in and out of lucidity all through that spring
and summer and one never knew how one would find him.
But today he seemed fine. The three of us discussed the
reading, and John asked Andrew if the publicity poster for
it would have his and my names on it. When Andrew
answered yes, John said, "Good!"—and then, turning to
me, added, —"because we can both use the publicity." The
circumstance of my standing unemployed next to John as
he passed out leaflets made his remark endearingly hilari-
ous.

In fact I had been surprised to be asked to read at all, since
the poetry scene was, as always, very cliquish. As the three
of us stood on the corner that morning, I felt an unexpected
warmth from Wylie, not so much in what he said, which
was more or less limited to details of the reading, as in his
willingness to linger in the goofiness of the moment with
apparent enjoyment, without words. The same radiance I
had felt when I was first introduced to him now seemed to
include an unusual benevolence, of which I felt myself to
be a lucky beneficiary.

After the Red Book benefit reading, Andrew and I began
to meet regularly and soon were putting together plans to
start a publishing house.

We wanted to do something specifically for our own
generation along the lines of what Ferlinghetti had done
for the Beat Generation with his City Lights Books. We
spent a lot of time talking about the poets we would publish and also decided that, like City Lights's Pocket Poets
series, the books should have a standardized size and for-
mat. We met at Andrew and Christina's Harvard Square
house (with its living room wall of books, mainly on history and politics), at our Belvedere Place apartment (I was
reading *On the Road),* and in the park with our babies.

Christina and Andrew's son Nick was around the same age as our daughter Strawberry.

In the midst of this, Andrew told Gailyn and me that he and Christina were going to be separating and would probably get a divorce. We were, of course, very sorry to hear it. We knew no other couple who shared our circumstances so closely. In fact, though, we saw very little of Christina. We also understood firsthand how exhausting and destabilizing having a family can be. Andrew told me he was going to move to New York and that the next step in our project was for me to meet with a friend of his named Victor Bockris, who would soon be returning from England. He would be calling me from New York when Bockris returned, and a meeting for the three of us would be set up.

3

That summer Gailyn and I tried to catch our breath and discover our new rhythm as a family unit, and at the same time tried to get a sense of how we might make our way in this new decade, still in the long shadow of the sixties. I met the poet Sam Cornish, who introduced me to the poet Ruth Whitman, who gave me a job in the National Endowment's Poet-in-the-Schools program, which she coordinated. The job would begin in September. One afternoon in July I got a call from Andrew in New York.

That evening before dark I was sitting on a Greyhound bus on its way to Manhattan. I was filled with a rare sense of anticipation, as if a new phase of my life was beginning. I had a copy of a City Lights book, Paul Bowles's tales about hashish called *A Hundred Camels in the Courtyard*. It was a book Andrew had recommended and the stories were brief and easy to enjoy and seemed to mingle with the mood of the coming night, the feeling of warmth and potential in the air.

Then I saw Andrew standing on Jones Street at night in the West Village at the lit entrance and under the sign of his new business, Telegraph Books. He'd been driving a cab that summer to make a living, and he'd taken to wearing a beret and a black leather jacket. Inside his bookstore and residence he had neatly laid out shelves stocked with a highly select group of titles from Heraclitus to Artaud to a few of our contemporaries. And here he introduced me to Victor Bockris, who turned out to be an energetic bantam-weight Anglo-American, a recent graduate of the University of Pennsylvania with a marked resemblance to John Keats.

The three of us had a wonderful night of jumping at each other with plans, jokes, major insights, more jokes, greater plans, coffee, a visit to a local diner, encroaching exhaustion, last-minute insights, more jokes, final semi-delirious exhaustion and passing out into makeshift sleeping arrangements in the store sometime just this side of dawn.

When you wake after such a night there is a momentary question whether or not the emotional investment — the equivalent of the three of us handing each other blank checks — will prove to have been an aberration one will soon regret. But as we staggered around and gradually got back into our worldly identities, I heard Victor's quick laughter and Andrew's intonation in a morning salutation I would come to think of as a personal signature: "Would you like some *coffee,* man?"

The three of us gradually began to be aware that somehow or other our luck might hold. Whether or not the projects we planned would fly, it looked like we all got along and were going to be friends. And that made the next morning almost as high-spirited and funny as the night

Seventh Heaven

patti smith

GOLD

Andrew Wylie

POEMS

Aram Saroyan

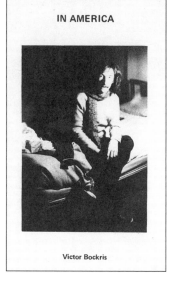

IN AMERICA

Victor Bockris

Telegraph Books Pocket Poets series, covers.

before. I gave the two of them a poetry manuscript I had
brought down with me called *The Rest.* Then I said goodbye and went uptown to catch the Greyhound back to
Boston. When I got back to our little apartment I knew I'd
made a connection that was out of the ordinary.

As fall began and I took up my duties as a Poet-in-the-
Schools at elementary and high schools in the Greater
Boston area, our Pocket Poets series began to be printed.
Victor had a working partnership with a printer outside
Philadelphia and handled the nuts-and-bolts work of seeing that the books looked the way we wanted them to:
mass paperback dimensions with a photograph, usually of
the author, on the cover. When the first copy of my collection, *The Rest,* arrived, Gailyn and I were both amazed at
the care and professionalism of the product. It was a real
new book we held in our hands.

After titles by Andrew and me, Victor went on to pro-
duce books by Tom Weatherly, Gerard Malanga, a memoir by Ron Padgett, Tom Clark and Ted Berrigan, and
Seventh Heaven by Patti Smith, her first poetry collection.
She had been recommended to Andrew by Malanga, and
Andrew, who had a quick eye for new talent, had been
immediately won over both by her work and her tough-
girl street style with its undercurrent of sweetness.

4
THE MOST EXPENSIVE WORD IN HISTORY

Perhaps this would be a good place to interrupt my narra-
tive to give my account of what turned out to be the most
expensive word in history. This tale not only casts some
light on recent controversies at the National Endowment
for the Arts, but also conveys a bit of the editorial vision
that informed the Telegraph line.

One night during the fall of 1965 — just twenty-two and having recently moved into a new apartment in Manhattan on West 85th Street — I wrote a poem. The poem* in its entirety, typed in the center of an otherwise untouched page, goes:

lighght

What does this poem mean? In "Ars Poetica" Archibald MacLeish wrote, "A poem should not mean/But be." I think this is perhaps a better characterization than any more lengthy interpretation I might be able to offer. But let me give it a try.

The poem is a variation on the word *light,* written during a period in which my generation in particular was exposed to a number of variations on the phenomenon of light. We were, for example, the first "TV babies," the first generation to grow up with television in our homes.

Around the time I wrote the poem, Marshall McLuhan, whom I hadn't yet read, was writing that in any given era the structure of the primary medium of communication — in our era, the television rather than the book — is so powerful it tends to make over the human mind itself.

How was the mind different in the era of "the global village?"

For one thing, in contrast to the previous era dominated by the book, our minds were now, according to McLuhan, less individualistic and more communal, since we had all watched the same television shows. Radio and television had, in effect, contradicted one of the fundamental truths of the previous era: that the same thing cannot be in two places at the same time. By putting the same thing — say "The Ed Sullivan Show," or even more to the point, "General Electric Theater," introduced by Ronald Reagan each

*From *Aram Saroyan* (Random House, 1968) © 1966 by Aram Saroyan. All rights reserved.

Sunday night — in a million different homes at the same time, television introduced and institutionalized nationally a sort of electric telepathy.

As a generation we had a more "tribal," perhaps a more "magical," sense of ourselves. We spoke of "tuning in" to things as older people spoke of "understanding" them, as if, like televisions, our minds were now a series of readily available "channels," receivers for a whole multitude of broadcasts. We were referred to as the "Love Generation," and we ourselves spoke of "Flower Power." As the war in Vietnam continued to escalate, we found ourselves polarized into a genuine counterculture. We dropped out, grew our hair long, and lived communally. We smoked marijuana and experimented with LSD. We created Beatlemania. All this, for better or worse, or more likely for both, was in full swing the evening I wrote the poem.

Why only a single word — and a misspelled word at that? Let me stick with McLuhan, who wrote that the electric-television era of communication has three fundamental characteristics: (1) It is instant. (2) It is simultaneous. (3) It is multiple.

A one-word poem is, in its own way, a structure that embodies all of McLuhan's essential characteristics and hence reflects the unique reality of the time during which it was made (which is, after all, at least *one* of the functions of art.)

It is instant. It has no reading process at all. The eye takes in the whole word as instantaneously as it would a photograph or the successive images on a television screen. If the poem were any longer, it would involve a reading process, and that would involve *time* — a beginning, a middle and an end — which, however contracted, would be patently uncharacteristic of electric structure.

It is simultaneous. And it is multiple. These two characteristics are perhaps easiest to observe together, as, for example, a television show being seen in a million different homes (multiple) at the same time (simultaneous).

In the case of a poem, once it is printed in a magazine or book, of course, it becomes multiple. But since magazines or books, unlike TV shows, are seldom experienced by two people at exactly the same time, the simultaneity exists largely in the realm of unlikely potential.

But this poem has an interior simultaneity, as if to make up for this — except for luck — missing element. It is the misspelling represented by the repetition of the *gh* in *light*. Having a double *gh* creates a structure both multiple and simultaneous (*ghgh*) in the poem itself.

A year or so after it was written, the poem appeared in an issue of the *Chicago Review,* and it was subsequently chosen to appear in the second volume of the *American Literary Anthology,* a book-length annual backed by the National Endowment for the Arts and supervised by George Plimpton. (The poetry judges for that year were Robert Duncan, Anne Sexton, and Louis Simpson.) This is where the trouble began and, amazing as it is to me, the source of it to this day.

Part of the honor of the poem's selection for the anthology was an award from the National Endowment for the Arts of $500 to me, as the author of the poem, and of $250 to the *Chicago Review,* as the magazine that printed it. This was a way, of course, to give support to both poets and little magazines. The program was to last one more year.

Representative William Scherle (R.-Iowa) brought the poem up on the floor of Congress in 1970 and denounced it as a misuse of public money at the rate of $107 per letter. Quite by accident, not long after this event, I met up with Robert Duncan, the poet who had chosen the poem for the award, one afternoon as both of us were waiting in Berkeley for a bus into San Francisco. I shared the ride in with him, delighted by his always fascinating talk. Among a great many other things he spoke of that afternoon, he happened to tell me how he had come to choose my poem for the anthology/award.

Duncan said he had liked a number of poems of mine that had appeared in little magazines that year — some of them more traditional in form — and that he might have chosen any one of them. The reason he had finally chosen the poem he had, he explained rather casually, was that an angel had told him to do it.

As the years have rolled by, I've more than once wished Robert Duncan had given a press conference when the controversy broke to explain in full detail how he had selected the poem. Duncan, after all, was the sort of talker one could imagine bewitching even the American press corps, and had he succeeded, we might all have learned more about why government should not attempt to interfere in aesthetic judgments, to say nothing of instances of divine intervention.

What I was doing in writing a one-word poem during the sixties has long seemed to me to be an equivalent in language to the work of Andy Warhol in painting (his instant, simultaneous, and multiple images of Marilyn Monroe) and Donald Judd in sculpture (his instant, simultaneous, and multiple metal boxes). And the works of these artists — respected and sold for large sums during the sixties — are now ensconced in major museum collections throughout the world, where they are properly regarded as integral parts of our cultural and artistic epoch.

My poem also entered the culture, but in an entirely different way. More than once during the seventies it was printed gratis in news and editorial columns throughout the nation, columns on the subject of cuts in the National

Endowment for the Arts budget. "Seeing the Lighght" was how an editorial in the *Washington Post* was headlined, an editorial that not only blithely ignored the poem's copyright but failed to acknowledge that it had been written by anyone at all.

And still the story of this one-word poem—or should I say its unrivaled fiscal history?—continues. When President Reagan forced new cuts in the NEA budget—slashes involving millions upon millions of dollars—he once again brought up the poem, by now a fiscal buzzword unto itself, to justify the move.

Finally, then, I must take exception, specifically and personally, to the use of this poem of mine, written in sincerity and honored in good faith by another poet. I object to the use of the poem, again and again over the past two decades, as the single most effective cutting instrument (when applied to the federal arts budget) since the invention of the chainsaw. This is not only tiresome; it is, in the most literal sense, *unen*-lighght-*ened*.

5

Now, to return to our story . . . It was in April 1972, after the car accident, which had left me without a car to commute to a term of Poet-in-the-Schools at institutions now spread far and wide across the state, that Gailyn and I and Strawberry, now a year-and-a-half old, ended up leaving Massachusetts and going to stay at a house in Philadelphia where Victor had a room.

The car accident disrupted our day-to-day efforts to come to terms with our new reality as a family, as well as our need to make financial ends meet. We were, after all, children of the sixties—more Flower Children than politicos—and settling down into a routine as a family was a big change.

The previous fall I'd stood in a long line at a bank in Harvard Square waiting to open a checking account, only to be told when it came my turn that I didn't have all the necessary papers. (A little later, that winter, I learned to drive and got the driver's license that is the accepted generic ID.) I seriously considered dropping the whole thing at that moment, but then realized I'd be paying every bill with cash or money order, often necessarily in person. That moment was definitely a benchmark on the road to reentry into the national mainstream.

By then, though, there wasn't much of an alternative. The counterculture was in pretty sad disrepair, a tattered remnant of its formerly spirited self. One evening in late summer we went to a party with the sports reporter George Kimball — we joked that George should have an ad in his paper, the *Boston Phoenix,* asking who else in the sportswriting profession went so far as to sky dive on acid — where we ended up talking with a former college football star, who had recently married. Dave Megessy had just come out with his book detailing drug abuse in pro football, which the former college athlete strongly seconded. Later on, however, Gailyn and I were unnerved when he suggested that we lend him Strawberry for an afternoon so that he and his wife could qualify for welfare. Our little baby? I'm not sure what it was, exactly, that disturbed me so much — perhaps just the impersonal calculation by which Strawberry assumed the role of fiscal prop.

So we pulled back and took the straight and narrow and even went out and purchased a little table-model TV, which, during that fall, fairly mesmerized us for a while. Hello, America. We ate a very natural, semi-macrobiotic diet, emphasizing whole grains and vegetables, with fish and chicken for protein. I stopped smoking marijuana, with the exception of a visit or two from old friends, when it seemed almost anti-social not to. I read Carlos Casta-neda's second book on Don Juan, *A Separate Reality,* with enormous interest and credence. But I also went to down-town Boston one afternoon to see, in the first week or so of its run, *Dirty Harry* with Clint Eastwood.

If opening a bank account was one signpost along the way to the national mainstream, I suppose quitting marijuana was another. When I was in my twenties, during the hey-day of the psychedelic era, for several periods of a few months each, I was a serious, even fastidious, grasshead. My idea of heaven was a stereo, a typewriter, a clean household with everything in its place, and a fresh-rolled joint of grass — a ticket to ride, if you will.

It puzzles me now to hear various spokespersons for the legalization of marijuana (and I believe it should be legal-ized, because then all of this would be uncomplicated by social pressure) talk about the drug's capacity to release one from America's consumer-oriented lifestyle. All my own experience points to marijuana being a drug that encour-ages consumerism. My friends at the time were all dedi-cated fans of pop music, for instance, and it was a standard thing to buy the latest release by The Beatles, The Byrds, The Stones, or The Doors, to name only a few, take it home, unwrap it, toke up, and let it be . . .

The character of time during this period was special, largely I believe because of my use of marijuana at regular intervals. For although it's a drug that relaxes one — at least this can be its effect if taken regularly — the nature of the relaxation is different from what comes out of, say, a care-ful diet. Marijuana produces a physical contraction that creates a feeling of energy and often delight — and also makes one seek out one form or another of psychic or spiritual or physical food. One contracts, that is, only to expand, in one way or another. All of us who have experienced the drug can recall the sudden desire for a sweet drink, or for music, or for a look at the mandala on the wall. And it is this need for expansion, after contraction, that gives time such a peculiar character when one is a grasshead. You must be very careful not to let arrangements made in advance interrupt your experience, in midflight as it were, and as the saying goes "bring you down." Hence one can become a jealous guardian of one's own pleasures.

And as this happens, there is an implicit distance put between oneself and one's pleasure and virtually everything else. There is the now-familiar prototype of the grasshead who greets one with a whisper and a look of complete gentleness, but this behavior is sometimes only the front side of a personality determined not to be called on for anything beyond another toke. It can be a behavioral DO NOT DISTURB sign, as anyone knows who has ever unwittingly tried to engage someone stoned in a conversation.

And as the distance between the outside and the inside grows, you find yourself going through significant parts of the day on "off." I would go out into the world with the sense that it was there for me to make my way through swiftly, in pursuit of whatever goods I was seeking, in order to bring them home and get high again and—implicitly the feeling was—really live. Hence, actual society becomes a sort of daily obstacle course, negotiated only because it supplies the goods needed for the next high.

So you find yourself getting selfish and intolerant, and you begin to notice how the day seems to get more and more like a series of deserts, relieved at the oases of the three or four joints a day you are smoking.* And to really be honest about it — anyone who has smoked for a while

---

*These are 1960s joints. Today's marijuana is probably ten times as powerful.

will confirm this, I think — although you could stop without experiencing the physiological trauma of withdrawal from heroin, you are for all practical purposes hooked. It didn't really surprise me that during a grass shortage in New York City several years ago, it was said that many users were turning to heroin for the first time, in lieu of anything "softer." One way or another, you need something.

And this is what eventually turned me off the drug for keeps — this, plus the fact that my own life was becoming too complex for me to deal with it and marijuana at the same time. Gailyn began it all, by stopping herself. Then she began to hate it when I turned on, when I left her for the other world, becoming too excited, too intense, for the actual moment in time — too *spaced out* of time, which doesn't stop even for the highest of highs. After we had our first child, things became even more impossible. There were continual demands, and they had to be met. As the family became a tighter unit, marijuana had to be excluded.

Finally I couldn't stand myself being high and looking at my own child's face, so open and so trusting and so giving, and all without the benefit of even a single toke of marijuana! The last few times I smoked, my guilt was overriding.

I became a two-headed monster, and one head looked sternly at the other, presumably trying to bliss out, and shouted DO NOT SMOKE GRASS!

So I don't. I go at the day now as if it were all one thing — one long passage involving ups and downs, yes, but not such heights and depths. If it goes wrong, it's OK, because there's always tomorrow and tomorrow and tomorrow. After spending most of my twenties as something of a Space Cowboy, I began getting back into Time.

6

But when we got down to Philadelphia in April of 1972, it was like falling back into a more tropic emotional clime. Victor had a room at the house of Nate and Bobbie (Bristol) Casto, and the couple generously offered us a room too. That first night at the dinner table a joint of marijuana was passed, and, though I was quitting, I herewith began a periodic hiatus on my abstinence for a couple of months, and breathed a sigh of relief. Sitting with Victor, Nate and Bobbie, it was as if we had found safe haven. Our reentry into the mainstream, then, wasn't a simple movement from point A to point B. In fact, since Gailyn and I were, respectively, a painter and a writer, it could even be said that we were trying to come to terms with society *for the first time,* since the sixties hadn't meant, for either of us, abandoning our former terms, but rather an underscoring of certain aesthetic anarcho-pacifist aspects of those terms. And to be in the presence of friends sympathetic to our particular paths was a reassuring respite for the moment.

Very soon, though, we began buzzing with plans to make Telegraph Books a bigger, bolder operation. Andrew — now entrenched in his costume of leather jacket, beret, and dark glasses — visited Philadelphia. And he had recently come into some marijuana of his own, which he presented as very special stuff. Victor and I smoked some eagerly, waited for the high for what seemed an unusually long time, remarked to each other and Andrew that nothing seemed to be happening and, just when all hope seemed to be lost, felt a sensation like having warm maple syrup poured over your head. It wasn't exactly a high, but there was definitely *something* to it, and with Andrew's enthusiasm we almost managed to convince ourselves it was very special grass — sort of Acapulco-Aunt Jemima.

Victor was in contact with the publisher John Calder of Calder and Boyars in London and he and John had discussed the idea of doing an anthology of the growing Telegraph stable of writers to be published by Calder and Boyars in England. It soon became clear that the next step for us would be to go to London to shore up this possibility. Perhaps, like certain rock stars before us, England would give us what America seemed reluctant to give: genuine mainstream support and approval. To raise money for the trip, we hit on the idea of selling the Telegraph Books archives of letters and manuscripts to the Special Collections Library at the University of Pennsylvania. The three of us visited Neda Westlake in her office there and spoke of the importance of the Telegraph effort. She graciously accepted us on our own terms and the archive was subsequently bought by the University Library.

We also spoke with Victor's business partner, the owner of the printing business that had produced the books we'd published, a middle-aged man named Frank who was sympathetic and full of enough good-natured credence to give us financial support for our English effort on behalf of Telegraph. In the midst of all this, Gailyn and I seemed to get our wind back from having a child and went into a period of revitalized romance. It was a lovely, green-edged, benevolent spring in Philadelphia, and life was once again the adventure it had been before we'd had a child.

On our way to England we stopped for a couple of days in New York, where we stayed at the Chelsea Hotel — Gailyn and I and Strawberry in a good-sized room on the tenth floor, Andrew and Victor in a smaller one a few floors down. I rented a car and drove with Andrew and Victor to Cambridge, where I retrieved some belongings I'd stashed in the basement at Belvedere Place and then drove back to

New York and put them in my grandmother's storage bin in the basement of her Park Avenue apartment building.

On the drive up and back, Andrew told us of the days of his late adolescence. He was at odds with his father, a blue-blood Bostonian who was an executive in the editorial branch of the Houghton Mifflin publishing company. At one point Andrew rebelled by going underground in Manhattan. He vividly evoked an Upper West Side brownstone with a lot of trafficking in drugs, sex and, if I remember right, guns. In this scene a woman he took up with one night turned out to be a man, an unnerving event, to say the least.

Victor, we had learned in Philadelphia, had only the most tenuous contact with his father, a well-known chemical scientist who had been a professor at the University of Pennsylvania and was currently living in Australia. His mother, long divorced from his father, had recently remarried and lived in Brighton, England. His closest relative in Philadelphia was his stepmother, an attractive woman who had been a scientific colleague of his father's and who generously put us up for several nights before we left for New York.

Andrew's candor during the car ride brought the three of us closer together. We had already begun to discuss the idea that if we could act in consensus, we exponentially increased our individual capacities and powers. Our meetings with Neda Westlake at the University of Pennsylvania and with Victor's partner, Frank, were successful illustrations of this theory. We talked about The Beatles, being four people, and The Band being five, as paradigmatic examples of this principle. The Beatles had changed the world. However, that we were not musicians in a group necessarily limited our arenas for testing the theory. I remember us working in concert, so to speak, all of us crowded into a small office, to get the secretary of a charter airline to book us on a certain flight to England. After hours of wrangling, we got our way, but it seemed a small triumph when so much power was at issue.

Another potential arena was an impromptu visit we paid to the offices of the *New York Times Book Review* to confer with its then editor-in-chief, John Leonard, a wunderkind not very much older than we were. We came to tell Leonard in person of our plans for the Telegraph line and to present him with copies of our three latest titles for review. Among these was a new book by Andrew called *Gold,* featuring a striking cover photograph of the poet in his now perennial outfit of beret, leather jacket, and black mirror sunglasses. It was a book of minimal poems that could be read from cover to cover in under a minute. Two of the poems were scatological. I was afraid that Leonard would be struck by the cover photo, open the book, turn directly to the two porno poems, read them, and begin to edge toward the door.

After Leonard consented by intercom to meet with us, all of the first part of my scenario, up to and including his opening Andrew's book and reading some poems, came to pass, and the meeting proved to be extremely brief and conclusive. "My field is the novel," I remember Leonard telling us with his eyes cast down into one of our books shortly before we left. There were no subsequent reviews.

We were, in essence, knocking around together, learning the parameters of the scene and at the same time keeping up each other's courage with our companionship. By this time most of the poets I'd been friendly with a few years earlier had gone their separate ways into marriages and families, and I was glad to have new friends.

We arranged to have a photo session at the photographer
Berry Berenson's 57th Street studio and invited all the
Telegraph writers we had published or planned to publish.
The photographs were going to be used in the Calder and
Boyars anthology.

That afternoon provided a wild conglomeration of
styles and strategies, from the old-line bohemianism of
Tom Raworth or Tom Weatherly, to the Warhol-linked
glamour of Gerard Malanga, who arrived in the May heat
in a coat with a fur collar, to the new punk hard-line of Patti
Smith, who was just a year of so from breakout as a rock
star.

Patti Smith dominated the sitting with a pro dynamism
that was as unmistakable as it was charming. There she
was, braless in an oversized Harley tee-shirt and black
pants, perhaps a hundred pounds in all. She was clearly
already a star; it was just a question of getting the message
out to the world.

During our last night at the Chelsea, while Gailyn and
Strawberry slept in our room, I met with Andrew and
Victor in their room to discuss last-minute details of the
trip. They had just seen *The Godfather* at Cinema I and had
been both impressed and shaken. At around midnight, we
heard someone calling down the air shaft their room over-
looked, pleading and moaning and threatening to do harm
to himself in a high-pitched voice. Andrew surprised Victor and me by reacting with genuine alarm, getting the
window all the way open and sticking his head out to
address the voice, which came from above.

"Are you all right?" he called out in clarion tones, looking up the air shaft, registering what immediately struck
me as a kind of patrician alarm, a genuine noblesse oblige.

The voice only moaned in reply.

Andrew pulled in his head, and at his bidding the three of us left the room to climb several flights of white stone Chelsea stairs to get to the suffering owner of the voice on his own floor. As we determined what floor that was, we passed Clifford Irving, a surprisingly tall and commanding figure, just then enmeshed in the Howard Hughes biography scandal, saying goodnight to some visitors at the door to his room, which turned out to be the one just above Gailyn's and mine.

When we got to the door we thought had to be the right one, Andrew knocked loudly, mobilized beyond any hesitation by what Victor and I suspected was misplaced concern. When there was no immediate answer, he knocked loudly again. Finally, a heavily made-up drag queen, whose mascara had run with his tears, answered the door and smiled shyly at the three of us.

"Are you all right?" Andrew asked in the same tone of stark Harvard clarity he had used downstairs a moment before.

"Oh yes, thank you . . ." the drag queen answered in a soft, apologetic tone.

"Are you sure?" Andrew probed further.

The drag queen nodded and after another moment we took our leave as he closed the door. It was, it turned out, just the sort of episode Victor and I had initially taken it for, but that didn't dim our admiration for our friend's sudden vigorous sense of citizenship. What I'm trying to catch here is the liberating suspension of judgment between us, fostered by friendship, that ran concurrent with the triviality of any of the exact circumstances.

All three of us were the sons of strong but distant fathers and we had each, in various ways, found ourselves brought up short by that circumstance and/or rebelled against it. Between each of us and the world at large there existed a certain suspicion and distance. What we found in friendship, I think, was permission to let ourselves be, and to go forth more confidently into the world. The iron-clad super-egos bred in us by our fathers began to soften and all of the stern pronouncements we were used to hearing inside began to be replaced by each other's approval and raucous laughter. For the likes of us, I think friendship of this kind was not only a great unexpected pleasure, a great gift of the world we had up to then jostled with with only sporadic success, but a literally healing process of transformation.

7

London turned out to be a lyric idyll despite the fact that nothing we planned worked out. We had sherry at John Calder's town house in a big, light-filled, high-ceilinged room. He glanced into Andrew's book, must have spotted the porno poems, and giggled. Nothing was clear-cut. Gailyn would mind Strawberry for a morning, an afternoon, or an evening while Andrew and Victor and I would psych each other up, go forth, and be met not by the brash American black-and-white of success or failure, but by a bland English-style irresolution. Perhaps we'll meet again in a week about this?

Our money was running out from the time we touched down at Heathrow. We were four Americans with a little baby in tow gambling on recognition and financial reward in an impossible time frame, three or four weeks. The innate impossibility made us semi-idiotic. Our first night we rejected the Hampstead rooms that had been booked for us by an associate of John Calder's whom we had nicknamed Henchman. The place didn't have the right vibes for our mission: storming the town. It was a low-key domestic rooming house, almost squalid.

We got a taxi and ended up paying much more money at a hotel in central London that night. Gailyn and I had a room on a lower floor and I could hear the all-night traffic around the hotel. She was exhausted; Strawberry was out of sorts. We ended up having a terrible, gut-wrenching argument. A woman caring for a small child needs a place to come to rest in.

"I can't stand it anymore," Gailyn told me, clenched and swallowing back tears.

The romance of the weeks before had suddenly, grotesquely shattered. In my years as a married man I've learned that each day is a new day, not necessarily stamped with the previous one's imprimatur of pain or joy. But I learned it slowly, glancing around charily to discover my wife engrossed by, say, a travel book when I expected the most baleful stare.

I grew up in an actor's bohemian household in Manhattan, everything quite warm and yet always unsettled about the future. (No actor believes he will ever get another job.) Gailyn, with whom I've shared this journey for over twenty years, is the child of a couple who chose a life in the American foreign service.

Both of us had precociously locked into the arts as a field for attention and concentration when our surroundings seemed especially precarious. When we met, during the "Summer of Love," I had been sharing the house in Central Square in Cambridge with a number of other young men for less than a year. It was far too long a time. I had the impression that no human being could ever understand me. Meeting Gailyn was like waking up out of a dimly lit, thickly plotted, mostly incomprehensible dreamscape into a new morning with the scent of spring blossoms on the air.

When we talked for the first time, it was like taking up a conversation that had been going on all along. I *recognized* her, as she seemed to recognize me. We could use short-hand with one another, whereas I had been tediously engaged for the previous months trying to get one simple point across. There was no point. Light and air and beauty and music had entered my life. I was the luckiest guy in the world that summer of 1967.

But now it was the summer of 1972, and after five years, on this night in a noisy hotel room in London, all that was over, finished. I felt terrible pain, panic. Somehow or other I finally fell asleep.

When I woke up the sun was shining, the traffic bustling below, and Andrew and Victor telephoned from their room eager to begin the adventure. First step, back by taxi to our Hampstead rooming house.

"Look, man," Victor said that morning. "I keep remembering some of this money is Frank's and I feel bad about blowing it this way."

We all agreed.

We had breakfast at a little restaurant perched on the corner of a steep Hampstead street where George Orwell had had his breakfast on many mornings. We visited John Keats's house, stared at his little lacquered desk, photographed ourselves in his garden. We ran and jumped, sang and shouted, and rolled down a grassy knoll on Hampstead Heath. My wife was looking beautiful and I felt happy again even while everything continued to be up in the air. I could look over at Gailyn, and her beauty would momentarily erase my dilemmas.

Then too, London itself was a reassurance. The minute we touched down we sensed there was something in the air here that had been lacking in New York. The taxi ride to Kennedy Airport had been hair-raising to me, no longer used to the erratic style of Manhattan cab drivers. The ride into London from Heathrow was a study in contrast. The big black cab was commanded surely and courteously.

After our first night in the central London hotel, I realized when we were back in Hampstead that I'd left a ten-pound note in our room. I called the hotel, offering a one-pound reward for the recovery of the ten pounds. I was put through to the cleaning woman in charge of our floor. She heard my story, went to check the room, and then came back on the line. "I 'av it roight 'ere, sir!" she told me in a chipper cockney accent. I wondered what kind of odds there would be of the same thing happening in a New York hotel.

The subway map available free from the station vendors was a model of clarity. The working men's restaurants we discovered served up excellent fare at reasonable prices. In effect, we were surrounded by a genuine civilization. As a result, even while our circumstances were fraught with anxiety, we found ourselves soothed and relieved.

One evening Andrew, Victor and I were to meet Henchman at a Hampstead restaurant. We would put the screws to him tonight. We needed money and we were going to get it. Now. He knew we were going to get it. It was to his *advantage* to give it to us, since then we would remember him kindly in our glorious, inexorable future.

We said goodbye to Gailyn outside what was now our basement room (while Andrew and Victor shared one upstairs). It was twilight, a blue twilight in the park across the street. Tonight we would bring things to a head. I kissed my wife in her pink turtleneck sweater and jeans goodbye.

We walked to the restaurant and took a table outside on the front terrace as the blue night fell. Henchman was late, and then he arrived with a kind of breathless, enthused politesse that was hard to get a grip on. How would we

corner the guy and give him the treatment: The famous
Bockris-Wylie-Saroyan, exponentially fortified, irrevers-
ible power drive? It was like dealing with a very slippery
social commando. The guy was English, and we didn't
know the style very well.

"All right," he said as we finished the main course. "Tell
me this. What do you want?"

It was night now. For the better part of an hour the three
of us had been wearing expressions we thought appropriate to wear in the presence of someone from whom we
wanted money. Our facial muscles were tired.

"What we want?" Andrew said aloud. Perhaps Andrew
was drunk.

"Yes. I'm a businessman." Henchman was forty or so,
tall, trim, and nicely dressed. "Just give me the bottom line
here. What do you need?"

Andrew, Victor and I searched each other's faces. My
mind had gone blank. The three of us had left the game in
the locker. We'd spent all this time hyping our power to
each other and forgotten to figure out what we genuinely
needed and a game plan for getting it.

"Twenty-five thousand dollars," Andrew enunciated
clearly, surprising me.

"Fine," Henchman answered briskly. "And what is this
twenty-five thousand dollars to be for?"

The three of us no longer dared to look directly at each
other.

"So that we can set up offices at the Chelsea Hotel,"
Andrew answered boldly.

Twenty-five thousand dollars for our hotel bill? To
forestall hysteria, I focused on my glass of water, concen-
trating on the little beads of water along the rim.

"Yes," Victor chimed in. "We do need to be at the hub of
the Manhattan scene, and I think we can make a reasonable
rent arrangement with the Chelsea management."

"Sounds good," Henchman said breezily, and now he stood up. "I've got another appointment, lads. John and I will be in touch ASAP."

What? He was leaving? We went through the motions of cordial goodbyes and sloughed back despondently into our chairs. Not only had we not gotten any money from him, he had left us with the dinner bill. Andrew stood up and went inside the restaurant to the bar.

"What's he doing in there?" I asked Victor, who now wore a drained look.

"Andrew? Man, he's cruising chicks."

"Oh."

Suddenly Victor came alive again and leaned across the table toward me. "Andrew was amazing just now when he said that about the twenty-five thousand dollars, wasn't he, man?"

"Yeah... I couldn't believe it. I almost started laughing."

"Yeah, well... But I'm glad he said that. I'm very glad he said it."

"Oh, I am too, man. Very glad."

"He's like a movie star, man, you know?" Victor continued. "He's got this heavy vibe."

"Yeah, I guess he does," I answered, wondering what significance that might have. Should Andrew consider a film career?

When I woke up the following morning, Gailyn told me Strawberry was ill, and that we had to do something, that the baby couldn't take the endless commotion we all kept stirring up to no effect. I suggested we call my aunt Elinor; I knew she would be good for a family dinner, a little emotional backup.

She turned out to be good for much more. The actor Rod Steiger was out of town and had left his Sloane Square apartment in the keeping of my aunt and her husband,

Walter Gruber. They graciously allowed us to use the apartment. There was no room for Victor and Andrew, but it eliminated our part of the rooming-house expense. We moved into a beautiful ground-floor apartment that opened onto a garden shared with the whole block of adjacent houses. It was the nicest place Gailyn and I had ever lived together.

My mail was forwarded and I received a letter from *Rolling Stone* about an article on poets they were doing. They asked for a brief poem and a photograph. I cut my face out of a photograph of Victor and Andrew and me that we'd had taken professionally in Hampstead. There was also a letter from Ed Dorn, one of my favorite poets, inviting me to visit him at his apartment in San Francisco if I happened to be heading West. I could feel California — six thousand miles away — in his letter.

One afternoon Victor and Andrew and I stood outside a phone booth in bustling Piccadilly Circus, debating calling John Calder.

"It's *going* to happen," Andrew told us, referring to the still up-in-the-air anthology. "Just call him."

"That's right, man," I said, gratefully focusing on Victor. "Just make the call."

"You want me to call him right now?" Victor looked uncertain.

"Victor, relax!" Andrew was hitting a new executive stride here. Positive thinking was the key. Just keep a good thought and the world was our oyster. "Take this coin." He handed Victor the appropriate one for telephone calls. "Put it in the slot. And dial John's number."

"OK. OK, man. I'll do it."

"No," I offered Victor, "he's right. We should give the guy a ring."

"Of course," Andrew said. "Just relax, will you both? He's going to print the anthology because it's very good. We're very *talented* and so are Patti and Gerard and Tom and Ted and Ron and Tom."

"And don't forget Tom and Tom," I added.

Victor laughed, Andrew smiled, and then Victor went into the booth and closed the glass door. It was a sunny day, unusual in London, and we were standing on a street in the theater district, where I had just auditioned for a part in the movie *Jesus Christ Superstar*. My aunt knew Norman Jewison and had got me into the audition. It had turned out to be a *dance* audition, and I had disgraced myself in front of the movie community.

Victor was now speaking, and Andrew and I were watching him, looking away, looking back. Then the call was over. Victor opened the glass door and came out making a gesture like an umpire calling a runner safe, his arms crossing each other and then moving out and then recrossing at the level of his midbody.

"It's over, man," he said. "It's over. The anthology's not happening, man. It's not commercially viable."

Andrew threatened John Calder's life.

"Cool it, man," Victor said to him. "He doesn't owe us anything. I mean he expressed an interest. We showed it to him, and he didn't like it. That's fair."

We went for coffee at a nearby Wimpy's. My own emotion was hardly evident. It was as if I was on a lark in London with my wife and baby daughter and two friends. Nothing was working out, but here were my two friends sitting opposite me, I wasn't in physical danger or starving to death, so I continued to marvel at our unfolding adventure. Oh, the world was large and mysterious and didn't bend to my will on command, that was clear. But then, how vivid it was! Since leaving Cambridge, all things seemed to have quickened in presence and heightened in color. See sun and try to think shadow, the poet Zukofsky challenged. But perhaps he was characterizing a very specific kind of sensibility here rather than pointing to a human universal. And if that—poet's?—sensibility draws so much from whatever is put before its field of vision, would worldly rewards be redundant? Yet we know from the lives of so many poets that, at a certain point, they are sorely, even fatally, missed.

When my friends expressed a strong emotion of disappointment, or hatred, as Andrew now indicated, my first response was surprise and then, defensively, humor. At the same time, if Andrew or Victor had done something that seemed genuinely wrong or unkind, I would have taken it as a personal betrayal. Then too, if I witnessed an unhappy child in the street, for instance, I felt piercing despair for the child and, abstractly, for the larger world. And if I was personally insulted, it weighed on me and could destroy the pleasure I would otherwise take in life for days, weeks, or months. In effect, I was both too impersonal and too personal in my range of response to things because I'd been too isolated. In marriage, I was learning about give-and-take in the most central relationship. With Andrew and Victor I was getting a sort of primer in the more worldly sphere with two neophytes of circumstances more or less parallel to my own.

We spent about six weeks at Rod Steiger's apartment, with its deep red walls, its comfortable bed, its air of solidity. I came across a note the actor had made in one of the books in his library: "People fall in love with each other's defense mechanisms." I found myself growing fond of this man I'd never met but knew from his movies—as an actor it's as though he says his lines to an unheard music—and now from the comfort of his home.

Andrew departed for New York. His gums were bothering him, which probably had something to do with that grass he still had. Victor moved into a Hampstead house with a lot of young English people. He had a brief romance with a young woman living in the house. One morning the two of us decided to hitchhike to Brighton while Gailyn and Strawberry stayed with my aunt in her Chelsea town house a few blocks from the apartment.

We arrived in Brighton during a sunny summer afternoon and managed to get to the house where Victor's mother lived at the crest of a newly developed suburban area, still quite deserted. She answered the door wearing a blue dress, a middle-aged woman with a strong physical presence, just this side of matronly, but with a vague, slightly haunted, nervous look in her eyes. It was as if her body had an instinctual understanding with the world but her mind remained tentative and uncertain. She greeted Victor with a kiss that seemed resigned and even perfunctory.

I was introduced and then we were invited from the foyer into the living room, where Victor's mother's new husband, a well-put-together man in his fifties, stood up from his chair and newspaper and greeted us. He was wearing very clean workman's overalls. It was quickly clear to Victor and me that we would be required to bullshit to pass muster here, and for this we fell back on a project the three of us had hatched before Andrew left.

I'd come across a wonderful book by John Buxton called *Byron and Shelley* and the three of us had decided that this book would also make a wonderful movie which we should write, and maybe even star in. (Victor, of course, would be Keats. Gailyn and I and Strawberry would be the Shelley family. And Andrew was Byron.)

The man Victor's mother had married was a cold-hearted old bastard who wanted to make short work of

these two American dreamers, and did. We sat there clink-
ing tea cups, nibbling biscuits and negotiating questions
like (to me after I mentioned I was a poet): "You make a
living at that?"

"Well," I answered, "we're working on the screenplay
and I'm also a prose writer,"—two lies that nonetheless
bore the seeds of my future.

The dispirited old codger harumphed his disapproval.
After about half an hour, Victor's mother saw us to the
door and we said goodbye. I walked out quickly into the
still bright afternoon in case mother and son might have
something more to say to each other. Poor Victor had a
broken family scattered all over the planet.

Several days later at the Chelsea apartment, I made a call to
George MacBeth, a poet and the head of the literary department at BBC radio, and made an appointment to see
him at his office. The night before the appointment, Gailyn
asked me what I was planning to say to MacBeth. I had no
very clear idea, thinking he might be interested in discussing the Telegraph Books project on the radio.

"Why don't you see if you can get an assignment?" she
asked me.

"An assignment?"

"I mean why don't you figure out an idea for a radio
program?" she said.

We discussed this for ten or fifteen minutes. I'm not sure
which of us hit on Bolinas as a possible subject for a program, but in another half an hour I'd typed up a one-page
proposal. I already had California on my mind because of
the *Rolling Stone* letter and the correspondence from Ed
Dorn. Bolinas was a little town in Marin County, across
the Golden Gate Bridge from San Francisco and then over
the top of Mount Tamalpais and down the other side. It
was around the lagoon from Stinson Beach. We had visited

Tom and Angelica Clark there a few years before and stayed the night. Recently it had become a full-blown poets' colony. Lawrence Ferlinghetti had a house there, and so did Robert Creeley. Joanne Kyger lived there, and David Meltzer, and Richard Brautigan had bought a house. Then there were younger poets of my own generation like Tom Clark, Bill Berkson, Lewis Warsh, and Lewis MacAdams. So I proposed a radio show that would explore the social and literary dynamics of this unusual community.

I met MacBeth in his office in the BBC skyscraper. We discussed the idea, I left him the one-page proposal, and he asked me to call him in a couple of days. He was optimistic. He doubted he could cover the air fare to California for me, let alone Gailyn and Strawberry, but he thought he might be able to put something toward it, in addition to a fee for a half-hour program.

By the time we arrived back in New York, Andrew was living in a one-room studio with a dirty picture window overlooking a Gramercy Park street, around the corner from Max's Kansas City. He had a very well organized door-table/desk with a small table-model TV on it. He insisted that Gailyn and I and Strawberry have his double bed in the middle of the room while he set up a cot for himself in the long corridor that ran from his front door to the main room. We were bowled over by his kindness. These were dark, rain-threatened summer days. We had very little money and had stopped in New York for only a few days on our way to California. Each night Andrew went to Max's and didn't come home until very late. Gailyn and I lay with Strawberry between us on the bed in the summer heat, listening to New York.

One afternoon I stepped into a health food store in the neighborhood. The young woman who came to ring up my items turned out to be someone I'd known in the city when I was going to Trinity. In those days she'd been a giggling, insecure Upper East Side girl with a very good figure, though she still had her baby fat. I'd last run into her several years before when she worked on the second floor at Design Research on 57th Street, where she'd greeted me giggling with a big kiss. Now she was more lovely for being lean, and the whole tenor of her presence had changed. We said hello; there was no kiss; we talked for a moment about the macrobiotic diet; and then she told me she was getting married in a week in New Jersey. She had lost the giggles and the baby fat and had turned into a serious young woman at the beginning of her odyssey. It was great to see her in the middle of that dark afternoon.

Andrew wasn't someone who spoke about the private side of his life. I saw that he was taking in New York now for all it was worth, living for the city. He and Christina were getting divorced, Nick was with his mother, and Andrew was at square one again. I couldn't imagine how it felt. I wasn't even curious about Max's. I had grown up with famous people — my father was a famous writer, my stepfather had become a movie star — and I guess I'd had enough of it all to last a lifetime. We never went to Max's during those days and nights but Gailyn and I both couldn't stop exclaiming at Andrew's generosity. Inhabiting his room and bed, it was as if we were the private side of his life, and Max's his public side.

On a Uwer borrowed from KPFA (the BBC's Bay Area hook-up), I taped an interview with Joanne Kyger one afternoon in July of 1972 in Bolinas. While she was speaking about the town's septic tank situation — the Bolinas mesa had as many as it could handle without violating health and safety standards, hence the town's building moratorium — it suddenly struck me that I was somewhere

I'd never been before. Here was this elegant poet who had studied with Robert Duncan, sat *zazen* at the Zen Center and been married for a while to Gary Snyder, but a woman with a kind of Bloomsbury sensibility, a slightly daffy quality, like a cross between Kay Kendall and Virginia Woolf, and she was suddenly getting down to literal shit.

"I want to live here," Gailyn told me later.

"Why? I do too."

"It's great. Isn't it?"

I was happy as much for her as for the place itself. We had had some strange times and it was good that these had led us to a place that called up all our best hopes again. It was like a sudden marital grace. Going from the night in our London hotel room, when everything had seemed to be over, to the afternoon at Joanne Kyger's house on the mesa, with its feminine clutter of books and beads and postcards and records, had been a matter of less than two months.

8

Bolinas made one feel not only that the sixties hadn't ended, but that they had gone on to effect fundamental changes in local government. Indeed, we arrived not long after a recall election had replaced all the long-standing members of the Utility Board—the town's governing body—with people of our own age, also from the East Coast, most of them from Harvard. Having known the poetry community in New York, I was given a warm welcome that felt oddly like a homecoming. We were soon ensconced in a rented house and I was writing long poems and then my first novel.

The town had a population of around 2,000 people and, after a few weeks, it began to feel as if you knew everybody. What mattered was that the community seemed

Gailyn, Strawberry & Aram Saroyan, Bolinas, California 1972.
Photo by Charles Amirkhanian.

happy to have another writer in its midst. I realized that as
a poet I had grown inured over the years to feeling, underneath everything, a bit like a social outcast. Now it was as
though I was not only a member in good standing of the
community, but even someone a little special. I soon knew
most of the members of the town's Utility Board as
friends.

If Andrew and Victor had, in a personal way, melted away much of the guarded outlook I'd maintained toward life, this little town provided a haven from which I suddenly began to write with a fuller voice, a voice at once more personal and more public. My first prose book was an autobiographical novel about the sixties called *The Street,* but, more to the point, it was written to an audience of my peers, those of us who had lived through the period together and absorbed its lessons and taken them to heart. Up to now, I'd seldom written anything longer than several pages. I was ecstatically nervous to be embarking on a novel. When it was done, I typed it up and mailed it to New York. I needed an agent.

It was here that I first began to reckon with the distance between the social and literary Shangri-la in which we lived and what was happening in Manhattan. Lynn Nesbit told me over the phone that she really liked the book, but wasn't sure she could sell it. I was too inexperienced to realize I was talking to the best literary agent in New York, who was expressing a positive feeling, and I needed to pull out all the stops and beg, borrow, or steal to get her to take the book. Instead, I played it casual and cool, Lynn sent it back, and I sent it out again.

When the book was published in the fall of 1974 by an alternative press and distributed by Bookpeople, I did readings in Chicago and New York to help to promote it. When I got to Manhattan, I stayed with my sister Lucy who had taken a good-sized apartment on Third Avenue in the Fifties. The night of my arrival, she had phone messages from Andrew and Gerard Malanga.

Andrew and Victor had, in the two years since we'd seen each other, formed a literary partnership, calling themselves Bockris-Wylie and writing celebrity profiles and interviews, primarily for the *Philadelphia Drummer,* a counterculture paper. Our contact had been fairly steady in the interim — we had been put on the mailing list for the *Drummer* so we could follow their pieces — but the fact was they'd been in New York for two years and I'd been 3,000 miles away in a little Northern California coastal town.

I remember sitting with Andrew at the kitchen table in Lucy's apartment that first evening in New York and feeling a mounting sense of frustration. His style seemed at once softer on the surface and more evasive underneath. It stung me when he said my book, which had been partly inspired by an abandoned autobiographical novel of his own, wasn't commercially viable.

The following evening Bill Knott and I gave a reading at St. Mark's Church on the Bowery. Lucy attended with her friend Berry, who had taken all our pictures that summer afternoon before we took off for London, and who in the meantime had married Tony Perkins, who also came. Allen Ginsberg was in the audience and so was Edwin Denby, the gentle guardian angel of the New York School, then in his mid-seventies.

Underneath everything, I knew the novel had been a big step forward. Afterwards, talking with Edwin Denby, who had read the book and was warmly complimentary, I even felt a moment of restlessness with the fineness of his attention as in the corner of my eye I spied Allen Ginsberg nearby. In a way, I was impatient with any overly careful posture of a writer when it might forbid him from jumping into his real work and swimming, as I now felt I had begun to do.

At the same time, I had seen people closer up in Bolinas than I had before, and I felt not nearly so clear-eyed as I wished. When I spoke with Allen that night, he asked me about a particular poem I'd read that he felt was too judgmental, assuming a divisive us-and-them stance. I was wrestling with that. Did one judge one's neighbor? Allen said it wasn't the correct thing to do. I no longer remember

Edwin Denby in his Chelsea flat, New York City, 1970.
Photo © by Gerard Malanga.

what my argument was—something about the universe
being a mirror—but I was perplexed. The question was
whether the writer was to step into the shoes of the universe—giving him a big voice indeed—or whether he was
just supposed to let the universe do its job.

There was a question in this about the next book I would
write, the second book, which in most cases is a hard one,

maybe the hardest of them all. When I got back to Bolinas, I would go into a long interim of twisting and turning with — and then finally letting my heart melt through — the quandary.

That night after the reading we went to a restaurant nearby, and I opted to sit with my contemporary Gerard Malanga instead of accepting Allen's invitation to me and Bill Knott to join him at his table. Our earlier conversation had been a part of it, I guess, but the fact was I was wary of any form of paternalism. Allen was, of course, in his fame as a writer, an echo of my father, and I wanted to stay on my own course and keep a distance from any, in Allen's words, "famous writer bullshit."

Now the friendship with Andrew languished for more than seven years. It wasn't until the summer of 1981 that I called him about *Last Rites,* a book comprised of a journal I'd kept as my father was dying of cancer that April and May. I needed an agent and knew he'd become one, working out of the John Cushman office in Manhattan. When I got him on the phone I tried to describe the book in the most commercial terms possible, and I could feel his reluctance on the other end.

"We're friends, and my representing you isn't a good idea. It could ruin that."

In reality, we had only the memory of our friendship. Andrew had spent the interim years exploring Manhattan's nightlife and every few years, like a bolt from the blue, I'd receive a message from him in the mail, as if his thoughts had momentarily touched down on our past. The most vivid of these was a very brief typed note enclosing a clipping from *Publishers Weekly* regarding my one-word poem "lighght," ever the subject of government controversy. The note, very cleanly typed in the center of a white sheet of paper, had a stark brevity. Somehow or other, though, a small insect had been crushed to death in the upper right corner of the page.

"Look," I coaxed, "just read it. If you don't want to represent me after that, we're still friends, OK?"

"Yeah, OK," he answered finally. "You'll mail it to me?"

"Right away."

I sent it off, already feeling relieved. I'd been through a round or two with a couple of other agents, Lynn Nesbit and Morton Janklow, and it was nice to be talking to someone with whom I felt a personal connection. Whatever the outcome might be, I realized there would be a human dimension to it, and that was something—win, lose or draw—I was going to appreciate.

Around midnight a few nights later, the phone rang. I had a premonition who it would be. Who else would call this late to a house full of children? After Strawberry and Cream, our son Armenak had been born on October 12, 1976. I happened to be up and quickly picked up the receiver of the wall phone in the corner of our living room.

"I love the book," Andrew told me.

He'd just finished reading it in the early morning hours in Manhattan. As with the call I'd gotten from him in Cambridge a decade before to come down and see him and meet Victor Bockris, I had a sense that a new phase was about to open up.

"You *need* an agent, man," he told me that night and quickly had me laughing. "You are the *worst* person I've ever heard sell himself. I didn't want to read your book after you described it. I thought it was going to be this sort of *Las Vegas* of the emotions."

A week or two later I was in New York to meet with him. I saw him first in his cubicle at the John Cushman office in the Chelsea district. He had lost most of his hair on top but wore nothing to disguise the fact and looked rather distinguished. He wore a tie and put on the jacket of his suit before we went downstairs to a bar for coffee.

By now I'd understood from friends that Andrew had gotten married again, but he still hadn't told me himself and I was wondering if he would. Sitting at a small table in the dark restaurant, he took a while but finally told me, and I congratulated him and chided him for keeping it a secret. It was as if his own life was changing again and he wasn't certain who among his friends would still be with him after the change. Eventually he invited me to his apartment at Waterside Plaza on the East River near Fourteenth Street to meet his wife and see Nick, who was living with them.

The apartment, which I saw that night, was high up and had a large living room with a commanding view of the East River. I stood at the window looking out at the nighttime view, thinking how far he'd come. Andrew's wife, Cammy (for Camilla), was a delicate, lovely Italian-American from the Bronx who had lived with him while he was taking amphetamines. She had helped him to clean up after he'd been arrested for a forged prescription. Here he was now with Cammy, embarked on a new life and career, having put himself back together. Nick came out to say goodnight, a freckled, redheaded Huckleberry Finn with very good manners.

Andrew told me that night that he related in a very personal way to *Last Rites* since he'd had a father a lot like mine. When his father had died in Boston, Andrew had been enmeshed in the underground speed scene in New York, stealing prescription pads from doctors' offices so he could keep getting his medicine. When he heard the news of his father's death, he'd felt an immediate unburdening and pulled himself together to make a trip to Boston. He wanted to visit the morgue where his father's body was.

Now he got up from the living room sofa where Cammy sat beside him and went to get a scrapbook, which he brought back and opened on the coffee table between us. The scrapbook proved to be a sort of patchwork chronicle of his life on speed, including as much memorabilia — ticket stubs, photographs, programs, etc. — as it did of his hard-edged, boldly inked script. He leafed through the pages and then handed it to me opened to a series of color photographs of his father dead on a slab in the morgue.

"Andrew had to have photographs," Cammy explained smiling.

"I needed documentary evidence. I had to make absolutely sure he was actually dead."

As wild and unnerving as this document was, I understood very well what he was saying. He had shown up at the morgue dressed up to make sure he would be allowed in to witness the great demon of his life, no longer in power. He had brought along a tiny, concealed Minox camera to preserve the evidence. He was admitted and shown his father's body and, somehow, managed to make the photographs, standing on a chair or a table to take some from above.

I had gone to the hospital in Fresno to see my father on his deathbed with much the same impulse. I had needed, most of all, to see his face as he was dying, to know he was indeed mortal. What had happened after I got to the hospital was an eleventh-hour grace and a revelation beyond anything I could have hoped for or imagined. But I'd essentially embarked on the same business trip as Andrew, bringing my younger daughter, Cream, along because I hoped she would help gain me a visit to my father's room (since he'd let it be known he didn't want to see me), much as Andrew had dressed with particular care for his visit to the morgue.

9
RITES OF PASSAGE

I got the telephone call on a morning in late June. It was from a law office somewhere — it sounded like a long-distance call, but I never made certain of that — and the man who spoke to me was making an inquiry on behalf of a lawyer, who no doubt had more pressing, first-person business somewhere else. It was an inquiry about a play of my late father's, the sort of call I get from time to time now. I referred him to the attorney for the William Saroyan Foundation. As the call was concluding, the man, whose vocal inflection sounded possibly Armenian, mentioned that he had just read my piece on my father in the July issue of *California* magazine. My interest picked up considerably. I hadn't seen the magazine yet; he had gotten an early copy by subscription.

"It's very interesting," he told me. Did I imagine he was hedging on a straightforward compliment here?

"Yes," I said. I knew it was interesting myself.

He laughed, perhaps uneasily.

Then he added: "The title is 'Daddy Dearest.'"

My heart did a sort of somersault that made me grateful I was on the phone and not facing the man. It took me a moment to restore a breathing pattern that would allow me to speak again.

"'Daddy Dearest'?" I asked, as levelly as possible.

"Yes," he said. "It's very interesting."

"I'll bet," I said, emboldened by the shock.

He laughed again. We never got beyond that word — *interesting*. Now that I think about it, though, he wasn't the worst sort of person in the world to break the news that you have added a tiny item to the luggage of that swiftest and most indefatigable traveler of our time, mass media. "Daddy Dearest" . . . I see.

Sorry about that, Pop.

William & Aram Saroyan, San Francisco, 1964. Photo by Archie Minasian.

Not altogether unexpectedly, Fresno, wherein reside apparently a number of *California* readers and where there are certainly more than a number of William Saroyan fans, took the article personally. There was an editorial in the *Fresno Bee* denouncing me. The local columnist hit the ceiling. There were several Armenians on the local television station's Evening News, talking about the bad boy I was for writing the piece. There were also many distraught letters to the editor in the *Bee*.

First a Fresno TV news team was going to fly up to the Bay Area to interview me on camera. On second thought, they decided to do it over the phone. We had a preliminary interview during which I detected more than an edge of hostility in the female reporter's line of questioning. My

father's name is on a very large building in the downtown
Arts Center in Fresno. The article, excerpted from my
book *Last Rites: The Death of William Saroyan,* portrayed my
father as a person of mortal failings. However, at the same
time all this was happening, other people were phoning
and writing me that they found the article compassionate
and moving. (The title aside, I thought the editors of *California* had done an excellent job of excerpting the book.)

By the time I did the interview that was taped for broad-
cast, I had decided to take a gentle tack. I would tread softly
and even apologetically. I realized, after all, that these people loved my father and, upset by the unfortunate title
California had given my piece, were rallying to his defense.

The reporter who conducted the taped interview, a man,
went about it less fiercely than the woman had, but there
was still an edge to his voice. He told me that a lot of people
were accusing me of capitalizing on my father's famous
name, of writing the book for money. Had I?

I said a few things about the book that were meant to be
indirect replies to that question. I had written it in a white
heat. I had never before had a book happen like this one. It
had been as close to being an involuntary reflex as I could
imagine writing a book ever could be. It had been written
in three weeks.

Had I written it for money? the reporter wanted to
know again. I sensed he was under a certain amount of
pressure to ask that question a second time, that the force
of community sentiment was looming behind him.

"No," I answered. I didn't say anything more.

The truth, of course, was less simple. For the first ten years
of the twenty I'd been a published writer, I wrote mostly
poetry. Then, after marrying and starting a family, I
branched out into prose. I wrote the autobiographical

novel about the sixties, and imagined I was going to make a financial killing. My father had told me again and again over the years that if I wrote a novel, it would establish me. So, at last, I took his advice and wrote one. Then for the following eight months I tried to get either an agent to handle it or a publisher to publish it. Though many who read the book seemed genuinely to like it, I was told repeatedly that publishers just weren't interested in the sixties anymore. It was the spring of 1973. I had a wife and a two-and-a-half-year-old daughter. That fall we had our second daughter. And still there was nobody who wanted my book.

I fell back on my poetry and small press background — "Don't kick down the ladder you stepped up," wrote the poet Louis Zukofsky — and the book was eventually brought out by a small outfit in the Berkshires. A nice job, but no money. However, my father now read the book, and liked it.

"It's their fault," he told me over the phone, referring to the publishers who had turned the manuscript down. Then he gave me what still strikes me — for the thoughtful room it leaves for future aspiration — as the best spot review a young writer could get from an older writer: "It comes close to being great," he said of my book.

"Thanks, Pop," I replied, delighted.

Next I did a biography of Lew Welch, *Genesis Angels*, and, helped along by the revival of interest in the Beat Generation, this one was published by a major New York house. I was given a modest advance, but it was still the most money I'd seen for a piece of writing. Then the book came out. And the critics hated it.

I had written the book as a kind of stylistic tribute to Beat writing at the same time that it told the story of the Beat Generation. Unexpectedly, however, it was reviewed the way Kerouac's own books had been reviewed when they appeared in the late fifties, with one exception. I didn't get the review in the daily *New York Times* that said this book was my generation's *The Sun Also Rises.* I really missed that one. But I got all of the others—the ones that were less reviews than they were character assassinations.

I developed a cough. I told Gailyn that the reviews didn't really affect me at all. But the cough wouldn't go away. I read about John Keats. He had gotten such a roasting from the critics on his first book that Shelley said it had killed him. My wife told me it was an honor to get such bad reviews—that only very good artists got them. We talked about the way the Impressionists had been first received in France. It was me and Kerouac, me and Keats, me and Renoir. But my cough still wouldn't go away. It occurred to me that I might have the initial symptoms of throat cancer. Perhaps I did. But thanks to the support of Gailyn, my family and friends, and of those readers who liked the book and wrote or told me so, after several months I seemed to recover my balance, and the cough gradually went away.

However, I made the decision not to do another book. I'd learned my lesson. I didn't want to die. All I wanted was to make a living. I took up screenwriting, a new ball game. Let my friends scoff and accuse me of selling out; I'd cry all the way to the bank. I would stay young while they grew prematurely crotchety, guarding their dignity and integrity, yet committed to nothing so much as dispiriting poverty. But I was going to have a life. The first script was written in a breezy two months. One draft.

And only one problem. It wasn't, in the end, a very commercial script.

The next script was different. It was a good idea, but it wasn't an easy script to write. At times, in fact, it seemed impossible. I did one draft. Then another. And then another after that. It's now in its eighth draft. And it's been optioned, but not yet bought. I've made a discovery. Screenwriting can be gruesomely hard work, and until a movie that one has written is made, one is not likely to be paid a lot of money for the work.

It was shortly after I'd finished the fifth draft of the screenplay that I got a call from my sister, Lucy, telling me that my father, from whom I'd been estranged for the previous three and a half years, was dying of cancer. And the next day I got another call from Lucy, now in Fresno, reporting through her tears that my father didn't want to see her — or me.

Around ten days before, after finishing the fifth draft of the script, I happened to have started a diary — more or less to take up the slack, now that I was off any writing assignment. With Lucy's second call, the diary turned into a marathon journal. I wrote six, eight, and ten hours a day as my father was dying. Since I had been told in no uncertain terms that he didn't want to see me, writing the journal became the means by which I tried to deal with the fact that he was dying without being able to know that reality firsthand.

The initial entries after Lucy's call were written in anger. Suddenly, for the first time in my life, I was allowing myself to feel the depths of my own frustration as the son of a famous man whom I knew to be quite different from his public legend. As I wrote these first entries, I won't deny that visions of a six-figure book contract danced in my head (over toward the side, as it were). After all, I was telling a story that the world didn't know about a celebrity. Indeed, it even crossed my mind that this might be another *Mommie Dearest.*

But as the days went by, my mood changed, and so did the book. It became clear to me, once I had vented my anger, that there were good and deep reasons why my father was the man that he was. It also became clear that the way for me to deal with my frustrations at being kept at a distance from him during his final days was to go see him, whatever the consequences.

The heart of *Last Rites* is the meeting I had with my father in his hospital room. The emotional culmination of the book was also the emotional culmination of our relationship, which had now spanned thirty-seven years. Had I not been writing the journal, I can't be sure I would have gone to see him at all. It was the deepening frustration expressed in what I wrote that enabled me to see the necessity of visiting him. My life and my journal interacted and, in conjunction, brought me to an entirely unexpected moment of healing with my father.

10

Andrew sold *Last Rites* while I was still in New York. Although it was less money than I wanted, I settled for it because there was action in the air. That year he and I worked on the manuscript, on the jacket copy, and on selling the first serial rights. He visited the publisher to check the cover proof and then called me in Bolinas to say he liked it. The book was one of his first significant sales as an agent and he seemed to be as excited about it as I was. Both our phone bills went crazy for a while, but there was no doubt on my side that it was worth it. When the tide starts to turn in one's life, the pleasure increases exponentially if you happen to have a friend along on the same wave. Maybe a third of our long distance bill was for laughter.

I was coming out of a long siege of being a family man and trying to develop as a writer simultaneously. In fact, the two enterprises seemed to be symbiotically related.

Bolinas was a kind of healing place, a crucible that gave me the space and time to work as hard as I wanted. It provided, with the pressurized piquancy of a small town, a wide spectrum of the Human Comedy. In the end, it was also a very hard place to leave. Gailyn and I had both begun to feel we had gotten from it about as much as we were going to get, and yet there wasn't money enough to make a break. But I could feel the karmic temperature rising in our lives, and Andrew in New York was a big part of that.

When the book was published, I steeled myself for another onslaught from reviewers. Remember, I had intended to give up writing books forever, to protectively gild myself with the big money in Hollywood. But then *Last Rites* happened, and I knew from the outset that I wanted to publish it. This was so important, perhaps, because when one is born into a celebrity's family, one hears so often from other people what kind of person the celebrity is. Since I was now reporting something quite different from what had been reported *to* me all my life, an essential part of completing the arc the diary began was to have it end up not on a shelf somewhere, but in that larger world that for so long had been telling me my father was someone other than the man I knew.

But the reviews worried me. For if my biography of the Beats had provoked such malevolent attacks, who dared imagine what might happen with a book that debunked my father's image as a sort of boisterous Santa Claus of American letters? It was worth it to me to suffer whatever slings and arrows might loom over the horizon in order to finally have my private truth made public, but it certainly made me uneasy.

But when the reviews began to come in, they turned out to be wonderful: the *New York Times Book Review,* the *San*

William Saroyan with his grandchildren, (left to right) Cream,
Armenak, and Strawberry. Bolinas, 1977. Photograph by Aram
Saroyan.

Francisco Chronicle, the *Los Angeles Times,* the *Washington
Post,* the *Philadelphia Inquirer,* the *Chicago Sun-Times,* the
Alabama Journal, the *Dallas Morning News,* and many more,
the reviews of a lifetime, certainly of *my* lifetime. And the
letters that came from readers were, if anything, even more
wonderful: lovely, deep, caring letters that told me what
was true of my father and me was true, too, of the relation-
ships many others struggled with in their own families. In
fact, the book seemed to reach both critics and general
readers less on the level of a celebrity exposé than as the
story of a father and a son, and of a passage in both their
lives when, at the eleventh hour, the two finally broke
through to one another.

Will the book ultimately diminish my father's name and
reputation? In my opinion, no. It's true, he doesn't emerge

from my pages as the bigger-than-life folk hero of his later persona, but it might be remembered that the public was never very drawn to that mustachioed legend in any case, as the very neglect my father suffered during the last thirty years of his career testifies. Whereas the man in *Last Rites,* though both troubled and difficult, seems to me a deeper, more complex, more compellingly human figure than his public image had ever allowed. I don't see how this could do him harm.

Likewise, the anger I released in the first part of the book now seems to me to have been only the necessary, initial step in an extended, and ultimately healing, emotional trajectory. For if, at the beginning, I myself entertained sly notions of "Daddy Dearest," in the end, knowing more of both myself and my father, I discovered I held him dear indeed.

II

Soon after the spate of good reviews, Andrew called and asked me what I wanted to do next. I said I wanted to write movies because there was no money in books, but we talked and I told him about a script I'd written, loosely based on my mother, Carol Matthau, and Oona Chaplin and Gloria Vanderbilt, who had all been close friends since they were debutantes in pre-World War II Manhattan. I'd just read an article about agents selling commercial book projects at lunch and thought the idea behind my unproduced movie would make a lunch sale as a book. He asked how much I wanted for the book, and I named a figure many times what I'd ever gotten, much more money than I'd ever seen.

"I'll see what I can do," he said crisply. "People are talking about you right now, so we have to move right away. Can you write something down on paper and get it to me?"

"Yeah, OK, but I'm telling you, I just read this article, and you can sell this at lunch."

"Just give me a couple of pages, OK?"

"Sure."

I wrote in longhand, filling up a couple of yellow-lined legal-sized sheets. The next step was to type these up, at the same time correcting them and editing them. Maybe I'd type up one more draft after that. But before I'd gotten to the typewriter the following morning, the phone rang.

"I sold it," Andrew told me.

"You sold it?"

He named a figure significantly higher than the one I'd asked for, and I involuntarily whooped and yelled to Gailyn. The kids weren't all the way out the door to school yet but there was a sudden singing going on in my blood.

12

It wouldn't be honest to end with an implied ". . . and we lived happily ever after." As I write, it is nearly ten years since that wonderful morning phone call from Andrew, and the ensuing decade has been in many ways an uneasy one.

I'd been blessed to find in Bolinas a place in which to grow as a writer and at the same time raise a family. When we left during the summer of 1984 and moved to Ridge-field, Connecticut, an entirely different kind of experience began for each of us. We had moved, after all, from a stronghold of literary Bohemia into the geography of the American middle class.

Sadly, by the time I was on the East Coast again, both Ted Berrigan and Edwin Denby were gone, and in the middle of the Reagan years I missed badly the moral and literary coherence that both men, in their different ways, proposed.

At the same time, I would agree wholeheartedly with Ted's observation that when people we care about die, they go from being outside to being inside us, where their spirit and value are perhaps even more accessible. I see things all the time that I know my father would find funny and share them with his laughing spirit. Likewise, I've found Ted's generosity to be sustenance in the present.

I've watched our children grow, and this has been, and continues to be, a great, if at times diffucult, odyssey. As our family matures, I recognize certain characteristics that seem to recur through the generations. For a sensitive tribe like ours — like most American families still in the midst of the shock of uprooting from one land and achieving a sense of home in another — historical touchstones have, I think, a certain value.

This story has chronicled the adventures of a young man lucky enough to come of age in America during the sixties. I say lucky because that time made one feel special and important, and I think ideally that's how the members of every new generation deserve to feel, and know that's not often the case.

"We were young, we were arrogant, we were irreverent, we were foolish. But we were right," Abbie Hoffman reflected in 1988. A generation born out of the Trojan Horse of the post-World War II American Empire, our power was, paradoxically, in our ambivalence about power. It was also in our numbers, and in the fact that our common ideals could foster friendship.